Dover Thrift Study Edition

Julius Caesar

WILLIAM SHAKESPEARE

DOVER PUBLICATIONS, INC.
Mineola, New York

Copyright

Copyright © 2009 by Dover Publications, Inc.
Pages 79–142 copyright © 1994 by Research & Education Association, Inc.
All rights reserved.

Bibliographical Note

This Dover edition, first published in 2009, contains the unabridged text of
Julius Caesar, as published in Volume XV of *The Caxton Edition of the Complete
Works of William Shakespeare,* Caxton Publishing Company, London, n.d., plus
literary analysis and perspectives from *MAXnotes® for Julius Caesar,* published in
1994 by Research & Education Association, Inc., Piscataway, New Jersey.

Library of Congress Cataloging-in-Publication Data

Shakespeare, William, 1564–1616.
    Julius Caesar / William Shakespeare. — Thrift study ed.
        p. cm. — (Dover thrift study edition)
    "This Dover edition, first published in 2009, contains the unabridged text of
Julius Caesar as published in Volume XV of The Caxton Edition of the
Complete Works of William Shakespeare, Caxton Publishing Company,
London, n.d., plus literary analysis and perspectives from MAXnotes for Julius
Caesar, published in 1994 by Research & Education Association, Inc., Piscataway,
New Jersey"—T.p. verso.
    ISBN-13: 978-0-486-47577-6 (alk. paper)
    ISBN-10: 0-486-47577-8 (alk. paper)
    1. Caesar, Julius—Assassination—Drama. 2. Brutus, Marcus Junius, 85?–42
B.C.—Drama. 3. Rome—History—Civil War, 43–31 B.C.—Drama. 4.
Conspiracies—Drama. 5. Assassins—Drama. 6. Shakespeare, William, 1564–
1616. Julius Caesar—Examinations—Study guides. I. Title.

PR2808.A1 2009
822.3'3—dc22

                                                            2009026176

Manufactured in the United States by LSC Communications
47577806   2019
www.doverpublications.com

Publisher's Note

Combining the complete text of a classic novel or drama with a comprehensive study guide, Dover Thrift Study Editions are the most effective way to gain a thorough understanding of the major works of world literature.

The study guide features up-to-date and expert analysis of every chapter or section from the source work. Questions and fully explained answers follow, allowing readers to analyze the material critically. Character lists, author bios, and discussions of the work's historical context are also provided.

Each Dover Thrift Study Edition includes everything a student needs to prepare for homework, discussions, reports, and exams.

Contents

Julius Caesar

WILLIAM SHAKESPEARE

Contents

Dramatis Personae

JULIUS CAESAR.
OCTAVIUS CAESAR,
MARCUS ANTONIUS, } triumvirs after the death of Julius Caesar.
M. AEMIL. LEPIDUS,
CICERO,
PUBLIUS, } senators.
POPILIUS LENA,
MARCUS BRUTUS,
CASSIUS,
CASCA,
TREBONIUS, } conspirators against Julius Caesar.
LIGARIUS,
DECIUS BRUTUS,
METELLUS CIMBER,
CINNA,
FLAVIUS and MARULLUS, tribunes.
ARTEMIDORUS of Cnidos, a teacher of Rhetoric.
A Soothsayer.
CINNA, a poet.   Another Poet.
LUCILIUS,
TITINIUS,
MESSALA, } friends to Brutus and Cassius.
YOUNG CATO,
VOLUMNIUS,
VARRO,
CLITUS,
CLAUDIUS,
STRATO, } servants to Brutus.
LUCIUS,
DARDANIUS,
PINDARUS, servant to Cassius.
CALPURNIA, wife to Caesar.
PORTIA, wife to Brutus.

Senators, Citizens, Guards, Attendants, &c.

SCENE: *Rome; the neighbourhood of Sardis; the neighbourhood of Philippi*

Act I—Scene I—Rome

A STREET

Enter FLAVIUS, MARULLUS, *and certain* Commoners.

FLAV.   Hence! home, you idle creatures, get you home:
       Is this a holiday? what! know you not,
       Being mechanical,[1] you ought not walk
       Upon a labouring day without the sign
       Of your profession? Speak, what trade art thou?

FIRST COM.   Why, sir, a carpenter.

MAR.   Where is thy leather apron and thy rule?
       What dost thou with thy best apparel on?
       You, sir, what trade are you?

SEC. COM.   Truly, sir, in respect of[2] a fine workman, I am but, as you
       would say, a cobbler.[3]

MAR.   But what trade art thou? answer me directly.

SEC. COM.   A trade, sir, that, I hope, I may use with a safe conscience;
       which is indeed, sir, a mender of bad soles.[4]

MAR.   What trade, thou knave? thou naughty knave, what trade?

SEC. COM.   Nay, I beseech you, sir, be not out[5] with me: yet, if you be
       out,[6] sir, I can mend you.

MAR.   What mean'st thou by that? mend me, thou saucy fellow!

1. *mechanical*] of the class of mechanic or artisan.
2. *in respect of*] as compared with.
3. *cobbler*] The word is used quibblingly in the sense of "botcher," clumsy worker.
4. *soles*] a favorite pun on "souls."
5. *be not out*] do not lose your temper.
6. *be out*] have worn-out shoes.

1

SEC. COM.   Why, sir, cobble you.

FLAV.   Thou art a cobbler, art thou?

SEC. COM.   Truly, sir, all that I live by is with the awl: I meddle with no
tradesman's matters, nor women's matters, but with awl. I am
indeed, sir, a surgeon to old shoes; when they are in great danger,
I re-cover them. As proper men as ever trod upon neats-leather[7]
have gone upon my handiwork.

FLAV.   But wherefore art not in thy shop to-day?
Why dost thou lead these men about the streets?

SEC. COM.   Truly, sir, to wear out their shoes, to get myself into more
work. But indeed, sir, we make holiday, to see Caesar and to
rejoice in his triumph.

MAR.   Wherefore rejoice? What conquest brings he home?
What tributaries follow him to Rome,
To grace in captive bonds his chariot-wheels?
You blocks, you stones, you worse than senseless things!
O you hard hearts, you cruel men of Rome,
Knew you not Pompey? Many a time and oft
Have you climb'd up to walls and battlements,
To towers and windows, yea, to chimney-tops,
Your infants in your arms, and there have sat
The live-long day with patient expectation
To see great Pompey pass the streets of Rome:
And when you saw his chariot but appear,
Have you not made an universal shout,
That Tiber trembled underneath her banks
To hear the replication[8] of your sounds
Made in her concave shores?
And do you now put on your best attire?
And do you now cull out a holiday?
And do you now strew flowers in his way
That comes in triumph over Pompey's blood?[9]
Be gone!
Run to your houses, fall upon your knees,
Pray to the gods to intermit the plague
That needs must light on this ingratitude.

FLAV.   Go, go, good countrymen, and, for this fault,
Assemble all the poor men of your sort;
Draw them to Tiber banks and weep your tears

---

7. *neats-leather*] cowhide or calfskin.
8. *replication*] reverberation, echo.
9. *Pompey's blood*] Pompey's sons.

Into the channel, till the lowest stream
Do kiss the most exalted shores of all.[10]

[*Exeunt all the* Commoners.]

See, whether their basest metal be not moved;
They vanish tongue-tied in their guiltiness.
Go you down that way towards the Capitol;
This way will I: disrobe the images,
If you do find them deck'd with ceremonies.[11]

MAR.   May we do so?
You know it is the feast of Lupercal.[12]

FLAV.   It is no matter; let no images
Be hung with Caesar's trophies. I'll about,
And drive away the vulgar from the streets:
So do you too, where you perceive them thick.
These growing feathers pluck'd from Caesar's wing
Will make him fly an ordinary pitch,[13]
Who else would soar above the view of men
And keep us all in servile fearfulness.   [*Exeunt.*]

Scene II—A public place

Flourish. Enter CAESAR; ANTONY, *for the course;*[1] CALPURNIA, PORTIA, DECIUS, CICERO, BRUTUS, CASSIUS, *and* CASCA; *a great crowd following, among them a* Soothsayer.

CAES.   Calpurnia!
CASCA.   Peace, ho! Caesar speaks.   [*Music ceases.*]
CAES.   Calpurnia!
CAL.   Here, my lord.
CAES.   Stand you directly in Antonius' way,
When he doth run his course. Antonius!
ANT.   Caesar, my lord?
CAES.   Forget not, in your speed, Antonius,

10. *most exalted shores of all*] high-water mark.
11. *ceremonies*] festival ornaments.
12. *the feast of Lupercal*] the Lupercalia, a very ancient festival of purification annually celebrated at Rome in February.
13. *pitch*] a common term in falconry for the highest stage of the falcon's flight.

1. *for the course*] as a priest of Lupercus, equipped for running at the feast of the Lupercalia.

	To touch Calpurnia; for our elders say,
	The barren, touched in this holy chase,
	Shake off their sterile curse.
ANT.	I shall remember:
	When Caesar says "do this," it is perform'd.
CAES.	Set on,[2] and leave no ceremony out. [*Flourish.*]
SOOTH.	Caesar!
CAES.	Ha! who calls?
CASCA.	Bid every noise be still: peace yet again!
CAES.	Who is it in the press[3] that calls on me?
	I hear a tongue, shriller than all the music,
	Cry "Caesar." Speak; Caesar is turn'd to hear.
SOOTH.	Beware the ides of March.[4]
CAES.	What man is that?
BRU.	A soothsayer bids you beware the ides of March.
CAES.	Set him before me; let me see his face.
CAS.	Fellow, come from the throng; look upon Caesar.
CAES.	What say'st thou to me now? speak once again.
SOOTH.	Beware the ides of March.
CAES.	He is a dreamer;[5] let us leave him: pass.

[*Sennet. Exeunt all but* BRUTUS *and* CASSIUS.]

CAS.	Will you go see the order of the course?
BRU.	Not I.
CAS.	I pray you, do.
BRU.	I am not gamesome:[6] I do lack some part
	Of that quick spirit[7] that is in Antony.
	Let me not hinder, Cassius, your desires;
	I'll leave you.
CAS.	Brutus, I do observe you now of late:
	I have not from your eyes that gentleness
	And show of love as I was wont to have:
	You bear too stubborn and too strange a hand
	Over[8] your friend that loves you.
BRU.	Cassius,

2. *Set on*] proceed.
3. *press*] crowd.
4. *the ides of March*] March 15, the midpoint of the month in the Roman calendar.
5. *dreamer*] visionary.
6. *gamesome*] sportive.
7. *quick spirit*] high spirit, liveliness.
8. *You bear . . . a hand Over*] The metaphor is from a horseman's domineering treatment of his steed.

Be not deceived: if I have veil'd my look,
I turn the trouble of my countenance
Merely[9] upon myself. Vexed I am
Of late with passions of some difference,[10]
Conceptions only proper to myself,
Which give some soil[11] perhaps to my behaviours;
But let not therefore my good friends be grieved—
Among which number, Cassius, be you one—
Nor construe any further my neglect
Than that poor Brutus with himself at war
Forgets the shows of love to other men.

CAS. Then, Brutus, I have much mistook your passion;
By means whereof[12] this breast of mine hath buried
Thoughts of great value, worthy cogitations.
Tell me, good Brutus, can you see your face?

BRU. No, Cassius; for the eye sees not itself
But by reflection, by some other things.

CAS. 'T is just:
And it is very much lamented, Brutus,
That you have no such mirrors as will turn
Your hidden worthiness into your eye,
That you might see your shadow.[13] I have heard
Where many of the best respect in Rome,
Except immortal Caesar, speaking of Brutus,
And groaning underneath this age's yoke,
Have wish'd that noble Brutus had his eyes.

BRU. Into what dangers would you lead me, Cassius,
That you would have me seek into myself
For that which is not in me?

CAS. Therefore, good Brutus, be prepared to hear:
And since you know you cannot see yourself
So well as by reflection, I your glass
Will modestly discover to yourself
That of yourself which you yet know not of.
And be not jealous on[14] me, gentle Brutus:
Were I a common laugher, or did use

9. *Merely*] entirely.
10. *passions of some difference*] conflicting passions or emotions.
11. *soil*] blemish.
12. *By means whereof*] in consequence of which misapprehension.
13. *shadow*] image.
14. *jealous on*] suspicious of.

To stale[15] with ordinary oaths my love
To every new protester; if you know
That I do fawn on men and hug them hard,
And after scandal[16] them; or if you know
That I profess myself[17] in banqueting
To all the rout, then hold me dangerous. [*Flourish and shout.*]

BRU. What means this shouting? I do fear, the people
Choose Caesar for their king.

CAS.   Ay, do you fear it?
Then must I think you would not have it so.

BRU. I would not, Cassius, yet I love him well.
But wherefore do you hold me here so long?
What is it that you would impart to me?
If it be aught toward the general good,
Set honour in one eye and death i' the other,
And I will look on both indifferently:[18]
For let the gods so speed[19] me as I love
The name of honour more than I fear death.

CAS. I know that virtue to be in you, Brutus,
As well as I do know your outward favour.[20]
Well, honour is the subject of my story.
I cannot tell what you and other men
Think of this life, but, for my single self,
I had as lief not be as live to be
In awe of such a thing as I myself.
I was born free as Caesar; so were you:
We both have fed as well, and we can both
Endure the winter's cold as well as he:
For once, upon a raw and gusty day,
The troubled Tiber chafing with her shores,
Caesar said to me "Darest thou, Cassius, now
Leap in with me into this angry flood,
And swim to yonder point?" Upon the word,
Accoutred as I was, I plunged in
And bade him follow: so indeed he did.
The torrent roar'd, and we did buffet it

---

15. *To stale*] to vulgarize, make stale.
16. *scandal*] slander.
17. *profess myself*] make professions of friendship.
18. *indifferently*] with impartiality.
19. *speed*] favor.
20. *outward favour*] external features, countenance.

        With lusty sinews, throwing it aside
        And stemming it with hearts of controversy;[21]
        But ere we could arrive the point proposed,
        Caesar cried "Help me, Cassius, or I sink!"
        I, as Aeneas our great ancestor
        Did from the flames of Troy upon his shoulder
        The old Anchises bear, so from the waves of Tiber
        Did I the tired Caesar: and this man
        Is now become a god, and Cassius is
        A wretched creature, and must bend his body
        If Caesar carelessly but nod on him.
        He had a fever when he was in Spain,
        And when the fit was on him, I did mark
        How he did shake: 't is true, this god did shake;
        His coward lips did from their colour fly,[22]
        And that same eye whose bend[23] doth awe the world
        Did lose his lustre: I did hear him groan:
        Ay, and that tongue of his that bade the Romans
        Mark him and write his speeches in their books,
        Alas, it cried, "Give me some drink, Titinius,"
        As a sick girl. Ye gods! it doth amaze me
        A man of such a feeble temper[24] should
        So get the start of[25] the majestic world
        And bear the palm alone.   *[Shout. Flourish.]*

BRU.   Another general shout!
        I do believe that these applauses are
        For some new honours that are heap'd on Caesar.

CAS.   Why, man, he doth bestride the narrow world
        Like a Colossus,[26] and we petty men
        Walk under his huge legs and peep about
        To find ourselves dishonourable graves.
        Men at some time are masters of their fates:
        The fault, dear Brutus, is not in our stars,
        But in ourselves, that we are underlings.

---

21. *hearts of controversy*] hearts bent on contest.
22. *His coward lips . . . fly*] The figure is that of a cowardly soldier running away from his colors or flag.
23. *bend*] glance.
24. *temper*] temperament, constitution.
25. *get the start of*] outstrip.
26. *Colossus*] the bronze statue of a man, 120 feet high, whose legs were so fixed in the harbor of Rhodes that ships sailed between them.

Brutus, and Caesar: what should be in that Caesar?
Why should that name be sounded more than yours?
Write them together, yours is as fair a name;
Sound them, it doth become the mouth as well;
Weigh them, it is as heavy; conjure with 'em,
Brutus will start a spirit as soon as Caesar.
Now, in the names of all the gods at once,
Upon what meat doth this our Caesar feed,
That he is grown so great? Age, thou art shamed!
Rome, thou hast lost the breed of noble bloods!
When went there by an age, since the great flood,
But it was famed with more than with one man?
When could they say till now that talk'd of Rome
That her wide walls encompass'd but one man?
Now is it Rome indeed, and room[27] enough,
When there is in it but one only man.
O, you and I have heard our fathers say
There was a Brutus[28] once that would have brook'd
The eternal devil to keep his state in Rome
As easily as a king.

BRU.   That you do love me, I am nothing jealous;
What you would work me to, I have some aim:[29]
How I have thought of this and of these times,
I shall recount hereafter; for this present,
I would not, so with love I might entreat you,
Be any further moved. What you have said
I will consider; what you have to say
I will with patience hear, and find a time
Both meet to hear and answer such high things.
Till then, my noble friend, chew[30] upon this:
Brutus had rather be a villager
Than to repute himself a son of Rome
Under these hard conditions as this time
Is like to lay upon us.

CAS.   I am glad that my weak words
Have struck but this much show of fire from Brutus.

BRU.   The games are done, and Caesar is returning.

CAS.   As they pass by, pluck Casca by the sleeve;

27. *Rome . . . room*] "Rome" was commonly pronounced like "room."
28. *Brutus*] Lucius Junius Brutus, the legendary founder of the Roman Republic, 509 B.C.
29. *aim*] inkling.
30. *chew*] reflect.

And he will, after his sour fashion, tell you
What hath proceeded worthy note to-day.

Re-enter CAESAR *and his Train.*

BRU.   I will do so: but, look you, Cassius,
The angry spot doth glow on Caesar's brow,
And all the rest look like a chidden train:[31]
Calpurnia's cheek is pale, and Cicero
Looks with such ferret and such fiery eyes
As we have seen him in the Capitol,
Being cross'd in conference by some senators.

CAS.   Casca will tell us what the matter is.

CAES.   Antonius!

ANT.   Caesar?

CAES.   Let me have men about me that are fat,
Sleek-headed men, and such as sleep o' nights:
Yond Cassius has a lean and hungry look;
He thinks too much: such men are dangerous.

ANT.   Fear him not, Caesar; he's not dangerous;
He is a noble Roman, and well given.[32]

CAES.   Would he were fatter! but I fear him not:
Yet if my name were liable to fear,
I do not know the man I should avoid
So soon as that spare Cassius. He reads much;
He is a great observer, and he looks
Quite through the deeds of men: he loves no plays,
As thou dost, Antony; he hears no music:
Seldom he smiles, and smiles in such a sort
As if he mock'd himself, and scorn'd his spirit
That could be moved to smile at any thing.
Such men as he be never at'heart's ease
Whiles they behold a greater than themselves,
And therefore are they very dangerous.
I rather tell thee what is to be fear'd
Than what I fear; for always I am Caesar.
Come on my right hand, for this ear is deaf,
And tell me truly what thou think'st of him.
          [*Sennet. Exeunt* CAESAR *and all his Train but* CASCA.]

CASCA.   You pull'd me by the cloak; would you speak with me?

BRU.   Ay, Casca; tell us what hath chanced to-day,

---

31. *a chidden train*] a retinue of attendants who have been scolded.
32. *well given*] well-disposed.

That Caesar looks so sad.[33]

CASCA.   Why, you were with him, were you not?

BRU.   I should not then ask Casca what had chanced.

CASCA.   Why, there was a crown offered him: and being offered him, he put it by with the back of his hand, thus: and then the people fell a-shouting.

BRU.   What was the second noise for?

CASCA.   Why, for that too.

CAS.   They shouted thrice: what was the last cry for?

CASCA.   Why, for that too.

BRU.   Was the crown offered him thrice?

CASCA.   Ay, marry, was't, and he put it by thrice, every time gentler than other; and at every putting by mine honest neighbours shouted.

CAS.   Who offered him the crown?

CASCA.   Why, Antony.

BRU.   Tell us the manner of it, gentle Casca.

CASCA.   I can as well be hang'd as tell the manner of it: it was mere foolery; I did not mark it. I saw Mark Antony offer him a crown: yet 't was not a crown neither, 't was one of these coronets: and, as I told you, he put it by once: but for all that, to my thinking, he would fain have had it. Then he offered it to him again; then he put it by again: but, to my thinking, he was very loath to lay his fingers off it. And then he offered it the third time; he put it the third time by: and still as he refused it, the rabblement hooted and clapped their chopped[34] hands and threw up their sweaty nightcaps and uttered such a deal of stinking breath because Caesar refused the crown, that it had almost choked Caesar; for he swounded[35] and fell down at it: and for mine own part, I durst not laugh, for fear of opening my lips and receiving the bad air.

CAS.   But, soft, I pray you: what, did Caesar swound?

CASCA.   He fell down in the market-place and foamed at mouth and was speechless.

BRU.   'T is very like: he hath the falling-sickness.[36]

CAS.   No, Caesar hath it not: but you, and I,
And honest Casca, we have the falling-sickness.

---

33. *sad*] serious.
34. *chopped*] chapped, disfigured with wrinkles.
35. *swounded*] fainted.
36. *falling-sickness*] epilepsy.

CASCA.   I know not what you mean by that, but I am sure Caesar fell
         down. If the tag-rag people[37] did not clap him and hiss him
         according as he pleased and displeased them, as they use to do the
         players in the theatre, I am no true man.
BRU.   What said he when he came unto himself?
CASCA.   Marry, before he fell down, when he perceived the common
         herd was glad he refused the crown, he plucked me ope[38] his
         doublet and offered them his throat to cut. An I had been a man
         of any occupation,[39] if I would not have taken him at a word, I
         would I might go to hell among the rogues. And so he fell. When
         he came to himself again, he said, if he had done or said any
         thing amiss, he desired their worships to think it was his infirmity.
         Three or four wenches, where I stood, cried "Alas, good soul!"
         and forgave him with all their hearts: but there's no heed to be
         taken of them; if Caesar had stabbed their mothers, they would
         have done no less.
BRU.   And after that, he came, thus sad, away?
CASCA.   Ay.
CAS.   Did Cicero say any thing?
CASCA.   Ay, he spoke Greek.
CAS.   To what effect?
CASCA.   Nay, an I tell you that, I'll ne'er look you i' the face again: but
         those that understood him smiled at one another and shook their
         heads; but for mine own part, it was Greek to me. I could tell you
         more news too: Marullus and Flavius, for pulling scarfs off
         Caesar's images, are put to silence.[40] Fare you well. There was
         more foolery yet, if I could remember it.
CAS.   Will you sup with me to-night, Casca?
CASCA.   No, I am promised forth.[41]
CAS.   Will you dine with me to-morrow?
CASCA.   Ay, if I be alive, and your mind hold,[42] and your dinner worth
         the eating.
CAS.   Good; I will expect you.
CASCA.   Do so: farewell, both.   [*Exit.*]
BRU.   What a blunt fellow is this grown to be!
         He was quick mettle when he went to school.

37. *tag-rag people*] rabble.
38. *me ope*] open.
39. *a man of any occupation*] a workman, a man of action.
40. *put to silence*] dismissed or executed.
41. *promised forth*] already engaged.
42. *and your mind hold*] and you still wish me to come.

CAS.   So is he now in execution
        Of any bold or noble enterprise,
        However he puts on this tardy form.
        This rudeness is a sauce to his good wit,
        Which gives men stomach to digest his words
        With better appetite.
BRU.   And so it is. For this time I will leave you:
        To-morrow, if you please to speak with me,
        I will come home to you, or, if you will,
        Come home to me and I will wait for you.
CAS.   I will do so: till then, think of the world.   [*Exit* BRUTUS.]
        Well, Brutus, thou art noble; yet, I see,
        Thy honourable metal may be wrought
        From that it is disposed:[43] therefore it is meet
        That noble minds keep ever with their likes;
        For who so firm that cannot be seduced?
        Caesar doth bear me hard;[44] but he loves Brutus:
        If I were Brutus now and he were Cassius,
        He should not humour me. I will this night,
        In several hands,[45] in at his windows throw,
        As if they came from several citizens,
        Writings, all tending to the great opinion
        That Rome holds of his name, wherein obscurely
        Caesar's ambition shall be glanced at:[46]
        And after this let Caesar seat him sure;
        For we will shake him, or worse days endure.   [*Exit.*]

Scene III—A street

Thunder and lightning. Enter, from opposite sides, CASCA, *with his sword drawn, and* CICERO.

CIC.   Good even, Casca: brought you Caesar home?
        Why are you breathless? and why stare you so?

43. *From that it is disposed*] from its natural disposition.
44. *bear me hard*] have a grudge against me.
45. *hands*] handwritings.
46. *glanced at*] hinted at, censured.

CASCA.   Are you not moved, when all the sway[1] of earth
         Shakes like a thing unfirm? O Cicero,
         I have seen tempests, when the scolding winds
         Have rived the knotty oaks, and I have seen
         The ambitious ocean swell and rage and foam,
         To be exalted with the threatening clouds;
         But never till to-night, never till now,
         Did I go through a tempest dropping fire.
         Either there is a civil strife in heaven,
         Or else the world too saucy with the gods
         Incenses them to send destruction.
CIC.   Why, saw you any thing more wonderful?
CASCA.   A common slave—you know him well by sight—
         Held up his left hand, which did flame and burn
         Like twenty torches join'd, and yet his hand
         Not sensible of fire remain'd unscorch'd.
         Besides—I ha' not since put up my sword—
         Against the Capitol I met a lion,
         Who glazed[2] upon me and went surly by
         Without annoying me: and there were drawn
         Upon a heap[3] a hundred ghastly women
         Transformed with their fear, who swore they saw
         Men all in fire walk up and down the streets.
         And yesterday the bird of night[4] did sit
         Even at noon-day upon the market-place,
         Hooting and shrieking. When these prodigies[5]
         Do so conjointly meet, let not men say
         "These are their reasons: they are natural:"
         For, I believe, they are portentous things
         Unto the climate[6] that they point upon.
CIC.   Indeed, it is a strange-disposed time:
         But men may construe things after their fashion,
         Clean from[7] the purpose of the things themselves.
         Comes Caesar to the Capitol to-morrow?
CASCA.   He doth; for he did bid Antonius
         Send word to you he would be there to-morrow.

1. *sway*] constitution.
2. *glazed*] stared.
3. *drawn Upon a heap*] collected into a crowd.
4. *the bird of night*] the owl.
5. *prodigies*] omens.
6. *climate*] region.
7. *Clean from*] contrary to.

Cic.   Good night then, Casca: this disturbed sky
         Is not to walk in.

CASCA.   Farewell, Cicero.   [*Exit* CICERO.]

Enter CASSIUS.

CAS.   Who's there?
CASCA.   A Roman.
CAS.   Casca, by your voice.
CASCA.   Your ear is good. Cassius, what night is this!
CAS.   A very pleasing night to honest men.
CASCA.   Who ever knew the heavens menace so?
CAS.   Those that have known the earth so full of faults.
         For my part, I have walk'd about the streets,
         Submitting me unto the perilous night,
         And thus unbraced,[8] Casca, as you see,
         Have bared my bosom to the thunder-stone;[9]
         And when the cross[10] blue lightning seem'd to open
         The breast of heaven, I did present myself
         Even in the aim and very flash of it.
CASCA.   But wherefore did you so much tempt the heavens?
         It is the part of men to fear and tremble
         When the most mighty gods by tokens send
         Such dreadful heralds to astonish us.
CAS.   You are dull, Casca, and those sparks of life
         That should be in a Roman you do want,
         Or else you use not. You look pale and gaze
         And put on fear and cast yourself in wonder,
         To see the strange impatience of the heavens:
         But if you would consider the true cause
         Why all these fires, why all these gliding ghosts,
         Why birds and beasts from quality and kind,[11]
         Why old men fool and children calculate,[12]
         Why all these things change from their ordinance,
         Their natures and preformed faculties,
         To monstrous quality, why, you shall find
         That heaven hath infused them with these spirits
         To make them instruments of fear and warning

8. *unbraced*] with doublet unbuttoned.
9. *thunder-stone*] thunderbolt.
10. *cross*] forked.
11. *from quality and kind*] contrary to disposition and nature.
12. *calculate*] foretell.

Unto some monstrous state.
Now could I, Casca, name to thee a man
Most like this dreadful night,
That thunders, lightens, opens graves, and roars
As doth the lion in the Capitol,
A man no mightier than thyself or me
In personal action, yet prodigious[13] grown
And fearful,[14] as these strange eruptions are.

CASCA.   'T is Caesar that you mean; is it not, Cassius?

CAS.   Let it be who it is: for Romans now
Have thews[15] and limbs like to their ancestors;
But, woe the while! our fathers' minds are dead,
And we are govern'd with our mothers' spirits;
Our yoke and sufferance show us womanish.

CASCA.   Indeed they say the senators to-morrow
Mean to establish Caesar as a king;
And he shall wear his crown by sea and land,
In every place save here in Italy.

CAS.   I know where I will wear this dagger then:
Cassius from bondage will deliver Cassius.
Therein, ye gods, you make the weak most strong;
Therein, ye gods, you tyrants do defeat:
Nor stony tower, nor walls of beaten brass,
Nor airless dungeon, nor strong links of iron,
Can be retentive to[16] the strength of spirit;
But life, being weary of these worldly bars,
Never lacks power to dismiss itself.
If I know this, know all the world besides,
That part of tyranny that I do bear
I can shake off at pleasure.   [Thunder still.]

CASCA.   So can I:
So every bondman in his own hand bears
The power to cancel his captivity.

CAS.   And why should Caesar be a tyrant then?
Poor man! I know he would not be a wolf
But that he sees the Romans are but sheep:
He were no lion, were not Romans hinds.

---

13. *prodigious*] portentous.
14. *fearful*] causing fear.
15. *thews*] sinews.
16. *be retentive to*] hold in or repress.

Those that with haste will make a mighty fire
Begin it with weak straws: what trash is Rome,
What rubbish and what offal, when it serves
For the base matter to illuminate
So vile a thing as Caesar! But, O grief,
Where hast thou led me? I perhaps speak this
Before a willing bondman; then I know
My answer must be made.[17] But I am arm'd,
And dangers are to me indifferent.

CASCA.   You speak to Casca, and to such a man
That is no fleering[18] tell-tale. Hold, my hand:
Be factious[19] for redress of all these griefs,
And I will set this foot of mine as far
As who goes farthest.

CAS.   There's a bargain made.
Now know you, Casca, I have moved already
Some certain of the noblest-minded Romans
To undergo with me an enterprise
Of honourable-dangerous consequence;
And I do know, by this they stay for me
In Pompey's porch:[20] for now, this fearful night,
There is no stir or walking in the streets,
And the complexion of the element
In favour's like[21] the work we have in hand,
Most bloody, fiery, and most terrible.

Enter CINNA.

CASCA.   Stand close[22] a while, for here comes one in haste.
CAS.   'T is Cinna; I do know him by his gait;
He is a friend. Cinna, where haste you so?
CIN.   To find out you. Who's that? Metellus Cimber?
CAS.   No, it is Casca; one incorporate
To our attempts. Am I not stay'd for, Cinna?
CIN.   I am glad on't. What a fearful night is this!
There's two or three of us have seen strange sights.

17. *My answer must be made*] I must answer (to Caesar) for my outspokenness.
18. *fleering*] fawning.
19. *Be factious*] form a party or faction.
20. *Pompey's porch*] a spacious portico outside the theater built by Pompey in the Campus Martius.
21. *In favour's like*] resembles.
22. *Stand close*] keep concealed.

CAS.   Am I not stay'd for? tell me.
CIN.   Yes, you are.
        O Cassius, if you could
        But win the noble Brutus to our party—
CAS.   Be you content: good Cinna, take this paper,
        And look you lay it in the praetor's chair,
        Where Brutus may but find it, and throw this
        In at his window; set this up with wax
        Upon old Brutus' statue:²³ all this done,
        Repair to Pompey's porch, where you shall find us.
        Is Decius Brutus and Trebonius there?
CIN.   All but Metellus Cimber; and he's gone
        To seek you at your house. Well, I will hie,
        And so bestow these papers as you bade me.
CAS.   That done, repair to Pompey's theatre.   [*Exit* CINNA.]
        Come, Casca, you and I will yet ere day
        See Brutus at his house: three parts of him
        Is ours already, and the man entire
        Upon the next encounter yields him ours.
CASCA.   O, he sits high in all the people's hearts;
        And that which would appear offence in us
        His countenance, like richest alchemy,
        Will change to virtue and to worthiness.
CAS.   Him and his worth and our great need of him
        You have right well conceited.²⁴ Let us go,
        For it is after midnight, and ere day
        We will awake him and be sure of him.   [*Exeunt.*]

23. *old Brutus' statue*] the statue of Lucius Junius Brutus.
24. *conceited*] conceived, imagined.

Act II—Scene I—Rome
BRUTUS'S ORCHARD

Enter BRUTUS.

BRU. What, Lucius, ho!
I cannot, by the progress of the stars,
Give guess how near to day. Lucius, I say!
I would it were my fault to sleep so soundly.
When, Lucius, when? awake, I say! what, Lucius!

Enter LUCIUS.

LUC. Call'd you, my lord?
BRU. Get me a taper in my study, Lucius:
When it is lighted, come and call me here.
LUC. I will, my lord.   [*Exit.*]
BRU. It must be by his death: and, for my part,
I know no personal cause to spurn at him,
But for the general.¹ He would be crown'd:
How that might change his nature, there's the question:
It is the bright day that brings forth the adder;
And that craves wary walking. Crown him?—that;—
And then, I grant, we put a sting in him,
That at his will he may do danger with.
The abuse of greatness is when it disjoins
Remorse² from power: and, to speak truth of Caesar,
I have not known when his affections sway'd³

1. *for the general*] in the interest of the public.
2. *Remorse*] consideration for others, pity.
3. *sway'd*] ruled.

18

More than his reason. But 't is a common proof,[4]
That lowliness is young ambition's ladder,
Whereto the climber-upward turns his face;
But when he once attains the upmost round,
He then unto the ladder turns his back,
Looks in the clouds, scorning the base degrees
By which he did ascend: so Caesar may;
Then, lest he may, prevent. And, since the quarrel
Will bear no colour for the thing he is,[5]
Fashion it thus; that what he is, augmented,
Would run to these and these extremities:
And therefore think him as a serpent's egg
Which hatch'd would as his kind grow mischievous,
And kill him in the shell.

Re-enter LUCIUS.

LUC.   The taper burneth in your closet, sir.
Searching the window for a flint I found
This paper thus seal'd up, and I am sure
It did not lie there when I went to bed. [*Gives him the letter.*]
BRU.   Get you to bed again; it is not day.
Is not to-morrow, boy, the ides of March?
LUC.   I know not, sir.
BRU.   Look in the calendar and bring me word.
LUC.   I will, sir.   [*Exit.*]
BRU.   The exhalations[6] whizzing in the air
Give so much light that I may read by them.
                                            [*Opens the letter and reads.*]

        "Brutus, thou sleep'st: awake and see thyself.
            Shall Rome, &c. Speak, strike, redress.
            Brutus, thou sleep'st: awake."

Such instigations have been often dropp'd
Where I have took them up.
"Shall Rome, &c." Thus must I piece it out:
Shall Rome stand under one man's awe? What, Rome?
My ancestors did from the streets of Rome

4. *proof*] fact, experience.
5. *since the quarrel . . . he is*] since there is no possible pretext for quarreling with Caesar
   on the ground of anything he is by nature (or has yet done).
6. *exhalations*] meteors.

The Tarquin drive, when he was call'd a king.
"Speak, strike, redress." Am I entreated
To speak and strike? O Rome, I make thee promise,
If the redress will follow, thou receivest
Thy full petition at the hand of Brutus!

Re-enter LUCIUS.

LUC.		Sir, March is wasted fifteen days.		[*Knocking within.*]
BRU.		'T is good. Go to the gate; somebody knocks.		[*Exit* LUCIUS.]
		Since Cassius first did whet me against Caesar
		I have not slept.
		Between the acting of a dreadful thing
		And the first motion,[7] all the interim is
		Like a phantasma or a hideous dream:
		The Genius[8] and the mortal instruments[9]
		Are then in council, and the state of man,
		Like to a little kingdom, suffers then
		The nature of an insurrection.

Re-enter LUCIUS.

LUC.		Sir, 't is your brother[10] Cassius at the door,
		Who doth desire to see you.
BRU.						Is he alone?
LUC.		No, sir; there are moe[11] with him.
BRU.							Do you know them?
LUC.		No, sir; their hats are pluck'd about their ears,
		And half their faces buried in their cloaks,
		That by no means I may discover them
		By any mark of favour.[12]
BRU.						Let 'em enter.		[*Exit* LUCIUS.]
		They are the faction. O conspiracy,
		Shamest thou to show thy dangerous brow by night,
		When evils are most free? O, then, by day
		Where wilt thou find a cavern dark enough

---

7. *motion*] impulse, prompting.
8. *Genius*] soul.
9. *mortal instruments*] agents of reason and will.
10. *brother*] brother-in-law. Cassius had married Brutus's sister Junia.
11. *moe*] more.
12. *favour*] feature.

To mask thy monstrous visage? Seek none, conspiracy;
Hide it in smiles and affability:
For if thou path,[13] thy native semblance on,
Not Erebus[14] itself were dim enough
To hide thee from prevention.

Enter the conspirators, CASSIUS, CASCA, DECIUS, CINNA, METELLUS
   CIMBER, *and* TREBONIUS.

CAS.   I think we are too bold upon your rest:
Good morrow, Brutus; do we trouble you?
BRU.   I have been up this hour, awake all night.
Know I these men that come along with you?
CAS.   Yes, every man of them; and no man here
But honours you; and every one doth wish
You had but that opinion of yourself
Which every noble Roman bears of you.
This is Trebonius.
BRU.   He is welcome hither.
CAS.   This, Decius Brutus.
BRU.   He is welcome too.
CAS.   This, Casca; this, Cinna; and this, Metellus Cimber.
BRU.   They are all welcome.
What watchful cares do interpose themselves
Betwixt your eyes and night?
CAS.   Shall I entreat a word?   [*They whisper.*]
DEC.   Here lies the east: doth not the day break here?
CASCA.   No.
CIN.   O, pardon, sir, it doth, and yon grey lines
That fret the clouds are messengers of day.
CASCA.   You shall confess that you are both deceived.
Here, as I point my sword, the sun arises;
Which is a great way growing on[15] the south,
Weighing[16] the youthful season of the year.
Some two months hence up higher toward the north
He first presents his fire, and the high east
Stands as the Capitol, directly here.

13. *path*] proceed.
14. *Erebus*] a dark region between earth and Hades.
15. *growing on*] toward.
16. *Weighing*] considering.

BRU.   Give me your hands all over,[17] one by one.
CAS.   And let us swear our resolution.
BRU.   No, not an oath: if not the face of men,
        The sufferance of our souls, the time's abuse,—[18]
        If these be motives weak, break off betimes,
        And every man hence to his idle bed;
        So let high-sighted[19] tyranny range on
        Till each man drop by lottery.[20] But if these,
        As I am sure they do, bear fire enough
        To kindle cowards and to steel with valour
        The melting spirits of women, then, countrymen,
        What need we any spur but our own cause
        To prick[21] us to redress? what other bond
        Than secret Romans that have spoke the word,
        And will not palter?[22] and what other oath
        Than honesty to honesty engaged
        That this shall be or we will fall for it?
        Swear priests and cowards and men cautelous,[23]
        Old feeble carrions[24] and such suffering souls
        That welcome wrongs; unto bad causes swear
        Such creatures as men doubt: but do not stain
        The even virtue of our enterprise,
        Nor the insuppressive[25] mettle of our spirits,
        To think that or our cause or our performance
        Did need an oath; when every drop of blood
        That every Roman bears, and nobly bears,
        Is guilty of a several bastardy[26]
        If he do break the smallest particle
        Of any promise that hath pass'd from him.
CAS.   But what of Cicero? shall we sound him?
        I think he will stand very strong with us.
CASCA.   Let us not leave him out.
CIN.   No, by no means.

17. *all over*] all in succession.
18. *the time's abuse*] the wrongs or grievances of the age.
19. *high-sighted*] haughty.
20. *by lottery*] by compulsorily drawing lots.
21. *prick*] spur.
22. *palter*] equivocate.
23. *cautelous*] deceitful.
24. *carrions*] corpses (a common word of contempt).
25. *insuppressive*] insuppressible.
26. *a several bastardy*] a separate, distinct act of treachery.

MET.   O, let us have him, for his silver hairs
        Will purchase us a good opinion,
        And buy men's voices to commend our deeds:
        It shall be said his judgement ruled our hands;
        Our youths and wildness shall no whit appear,
        But all be buried in his gravity.

BRU.   O, name him not: let us not break[27] with him,
        For he will never follow any thing
        That other men begin.

CAS.   Then leave him out.

CASCA.   Indeed he is not fit.

DEC.   Shall no man else be touch'd but only Caesar?

CAS.   Decius, well urged: I think it is not meet
        Mark Antony, so well beloved of Caesar,
        Should outlive Caesar: we shall find of him
        A shrewd contriver; and you know his means,
        If he improve them, may well stretch so far
        As to annoy[28] us all: which to prevent,
        Let Antony and Caesar fall together.

BRU.   Our course will seem too bloody, Caius Cassius,
        To cut the head off and then hack the limbs,
        Like wrath in death and envy[29] afterwards;
        For Antony is but a limb of Caesar:
        Let us be sacrificers, but not butchers, Caius.
        We all stand up against the spirit of Caesar,
        And in the spirit of men there is no blood:
        O, that we then could come by Caesar's spirit,
        And not dismember Caesar! But, alas,
        Caesar must bleed for it! And, gentle friends,
        Let's kill him boldly, but not wrathfully;
        Let's carve him as a dish fit for the gods,
        Not hew him as a carcass fit for hounds:
        And let our hearts, as subtle masters do,
        Stir up their servants to an act of rage
        And after seem to chide 'em. This shall make
        Our purpose necessary and not envious:[30]
        Which so appearing to the common eyes,
        We shall be call'd purgers, not murderers.

27. *break*] communicate.
28. *annoy*] harm.
29. *envy*] malice.
30. *envious*] malicious.

                    And for Mark Antony, think not of him;
                    For he can do no more than Caesar's arm
                    When Caesar's head is off.
CAS.   Yet I fear him,
                    For in the ingrafted love he bears to Caesar—
BRU.   Alas, good Cassius, do not think of him:
                    If he love Caesar, all that he can do
                    Is to himself, take thought[31] and die for Caesar:
                    And that were much he should,[32] for he is given
                    To sports, to wildness and much company.
TREB.   There is no fear[33] in him; let him not die;
                    For he will live and laugh at this hereafter.   [*Clock strikes.*]
BRU.   Peace! count the clock.
CAS.   The clock hath stricken three.
TREB.   'T is time to part.
CAS.   But it is doubtful yet
                    Whether Caesar will come forth to-day or no;
                    For he is superstitious grown of late,
                    Quite from the main opinion[34] he held once
                    Of fantasy, of dreams and ceremonies:[35]
                    It may be these apparent prodigies,
                    The unaccustom'd terror of this night
                    And the persuasion of his augurers,
                    May hold him from the Capitol to-day.
DEC.   Never fear that: if he be so resolved,
                    I can o'ersway him; for he loves to hear
                    That unicorns may be betray'd with trees
                    And bears with glasses,[36] elephants with holes,
                    Lions with toils[37] and men with flatterers:
                    But when I tell him he hates flatterers,
                    He says he does, being then most flattered.
                    Let me work;
                    For I can give his humour the true bent,
                    And I will bring him to the Capitol.

31. *take thought*] grieve.
32. *that were much he should*] that would be difficult for him.
33. *no fear*] nothing to fear.
34. *from the main opinion*] contrary to the firm opinion.
35. *ceremonies*] omens.
36. *glasses*] mirrors.
37. *toils*] nets.

CAS.   Nay, we will all of us be there to fetch him.
BRU.   By the eighth hour: is that the uttermost?[38]
CIN.   Be that the uttermost, and fail not then.
MET.   Caius Ligarius doth bear Caesar hard,
            Who rated him for speaking well of Pompey:
            I wonder none of you have thought of him.
BRU.   Now, good Metellus, go along by him:
            He loves me well, and I have given him reasons;
            Send him but hither, and I'll fashion him.
CAS.   The morning comes upon 's: we'll leave you, Brutus:
            And, friends, disperse yourselves: but all remember
            What you have said and show yourselves true Romans.
BRU.   Good gentlemen, look fresh and merrily;
            Let not our looks put on[39] our purposes;
            But bear it as our Roman actors do,
            With untired spirits and formal constancy:[40]
            And so, good morrow to you every one. [*Exeunt all but* BRUTUS.]
            Boy! Lucius! Fast asleep! It is no matter;
            Enjoy the honey-heavy dew of slumber:
            Thou hast no figures[41] nor no fantasies,
            Which busy care draws in the brains of men;
            Therefore thou sleep'st so sound.

Enter PORTIA.

POR.   Brutus, my lord!
BRU.   Portia, what mean you? wherefore rise you now?
            It is not for your health thus to commit
            Your weak condition to the raw cold morning.
POR.   Nor for yours neither. You've ungently, Brutus,
            Stole from my bed: and yesternight at supper
            You suddenly arose and walk'd about,
            Musing and sighing, with your arms across;
            And when I ask'd you what the matter was,
            You stared upon me with ungentle looks:
            I urged you further; then you scratch'd your head,
            And too impatiently stamp'd with your foot:
            Yet I insisted, yet you answer'd not,

38. *uttermost*] latest.
39. *put on*] reveal.
40. *formal constancy*] consistent dignity.
41. *figures*] vain fancies.

But with an angry wafture[42] of your hand
Gave sign for me to leave you: so I did,
Fearing to strengthen that impatience
Which seem'd too much enkindled, and withal
Hoping it was but an effect of humour,[43]
Which sometime hath his hour with every man.
It will not let you eat, nor talk, nor sleep,
And, could it work so much upon your shape
As it hath much prevail'd on your condition,[44]
I should not know you, Brutus. Dear my lord,
Make me acquainted with your cause of grief.

BRU. I am not well in health, and that is all.

POR. Brutus is wise, and, were he not in health,
He would embrace the means to come by it.

BRU. Why, so I do: good Portia, go to bed.

POR. Is Brutus sick, and is it physical[45]
To walk unbraced and suck up the humours
Of the dank morning? What, is Brutus sick,
And will he steal out of his wholesome bed,
To dare the vile contagion of the night,
And tempt the rheumy and unpurged[46] air
To add unto his sickness? No, my Brutus;
You have some sick offence[47] within your mind,
Which by the right and virtue of my place
I ought to know of: and, upon my knees,
I charm[48] you, by my once commended beauty,
By all your vows of love and that great vow
Which did incorporate and make us one,
That you unfold to me, yourself, your half,
Why you are heavy, and what men to-night
Have had resort to you; for here have been
Some six or seven, who did hide their faces
Even from darkness.

BRU.   Kneel not, gentle Portia.

POR. I should not need, if you were gentle Brutus.

42. *wafture*] wave.
43. *humour*] caprice.
44. *condition*] disposition.
45. *physical*] wholesome.
46. *rheumy and unpurged*] damp and impure.
47. *sick offence*] morbid obstruction.
48. *charm*] adjure.

Within the bond of marriage, tell me, Brutus,
Is it excepted I should know no secrets
That appertain to you? Am I yourself
But, as it were, in sort or limitation,
To keep with you at meals, comfort your bed,
And talk to you sometimes? Dwell I but in the suburbs
Of your good pleasure? If it be no more,
Portia is Brutus' harlot, not his wife.

BRU. You are my true and honourable wife,
As dear to me as are the ruddy drops
That visit my sad heart.

POR. If this were true, then should I know this secret.
I grant I am a woman, but withal
A woman that Lord Brutus took to wife:
I grant I am a woman, but withal
A woman well reputed, Cato's daughter.
Think you I am no stronger than my sex,
Being so father'd and so husbanded?
Tell me your counsels, I will not disclose 'em:
I have made strong proof of my constancy,
Giving myself a voluntary wound
Here in the thigh: can I bear that with patience
And not my husband's secrets?

BRU.   O ye gods,
Render me worthy of this noble wife!   [Knocking within.]
Hark, hark! one knocks: Portia, go in a while;
And by and by thy bosom shall partake
The secrets of my heart:
All my engagements I will construe to thee,
All the charactery[49] of my sad brows.
Leave me with haste. [Exit PORTIA.] Lucius, who's that knocks?

Re-enter LUCIUS with LIGARIUS.

LUC. Here is a sick man that would speak with you.
BRU. Caius Ligarius, that Metellus spake of.
Boy, stand aside. Caius Ligarius! how?
LIG. Vouchsafe[50] good morrow from a feeble tongue.
BRU. O, what a time have you chose out, brave Caius,

---

49. *charactery*] written symbols.
50. *Vouchsafe*] deign to accept.

	To wear a kerchief![51] Would you were not sick!
LIG.	I am not sick, if Brutus have in hand
	Any exploit worthy the name of honour.
BRU.	Such an exploit have I in hand, Ligarius,
	Had you a healthful ear to hear of it.
LIG.	By all the gods that Romans bow before,
	I here discard my sickness! Soul of Rome!
	Brave son, derived from honourable loins!
	Thou, like an exorcist,[52] hast conjured up
	My mortified[53] spirit. Now bid me run,
	And I will strive with things impossible,
	Yea, get the better of them. What's to do?
BRU.	A piece of work that will make sick men whole.
LIG.	But are not some whole that we must make sick?
BRU.	That must we also. What it is, my Caius,
	I shall unfold to thee, as we are going
	To whom it must be done.
LIG.	Set on your foot,
	And with a heart new-fired I follow you,
	To do I know not what: but it sufficeth
	That Brutus leads me on.
BRU.	Follow me then. [*Exeunt.*]

Scene II—Caesar's house

Thunder and lightning. Enter CAESAR, *in his night-gown.*

CAES.	Nor heaven nor earth have been at peace to-night:
	Thrice hath Calpurnia in her sleep cried out,
	"Help, ho! they murder Caesar!" Who's within?

Enter a Servant.

SERV.	My lord?
CAES.	Go bid the priests do present sacrifice,
	And bring me their opinions of success.[1]

51. *To wear a kerchief*] a common mode of treating illness.
52. *exorcist*] one who raises spirits.
53. *mortified*] dead.

1. *success*] the result.

SERV.   I will, my lord.   *[Exit.]*

Enter CALPURNIA.

CAL.   What mean you, Caesar? think you to walk forth?
       You shall not stir out of your house to-day.

CAES.   Caesar shall forth: the things that threaten'd me
       Ne'er look'd but on my back; when they shall see
       The face of Caesar, they are vanished.

CAL.   Caesar, I never stood on ceremonies,[2]
       Yet now they fright me. There is one within,
       Besides the things that we have heard and seen,
       Recounts most horrid sights seen by the watch.
       A lioness hath whelped in the streets;
       And graves have yawn'd, and yielded up their dead;
       Fierce fiery warriors fight upon the clouds,
       In ranks and squadrons and right form of war,
       Which drizzled blood upon the Capitol;
       The noise of battle hurtled in the air,
       Horses did neigh and dying men did groan,
       And ghosts did shriek and squeal about the streets.
       O Caesar! these things are beyond all use,
       And I do fear them.

CAES.   What can be avoided
       Whose end is purposed by the mighty gods?
       Yet Caesar shall go forth; for these predictions
       Are to the world in general as to Caesar.

CAL.   When beggars die, there are no comets seen;
       The heavens themselves blaze forth the death of princes.

CAES.   Cowards die many times before their deaths;
       The valiant never taste of death but once.
       Of all the wonders that I yet have heard,
       It seems to me most strange that men should fear;
       Seeing that death, a necessary end,
       Will come when it will come.

Re-enter Servant.

                            What say the augurers?

SERV.   They would not have you to stir forth to-day.
       Plucking the entrails of an offering forth,
       They could not find a heart within the beast.

CAES.   The gods do this in shame of cowardice:

---

2. *stood on ceremonies*] attached importance to omens.

1

Caesar should be a beast without a heart
If he should stay at home to-day for fear.
No, Caesar shall not: danger knows full well
That Caesar is more dangerous than he:
We are two lions litter'd in one day,
And I the elder and more terrible:
And Caesar shall go forth.

CAL.   Alas, my lord,
Your wisdom is consumed in confidence.
Do not go forth to-day: call it my fear
That keeps you in the house and not your own.
We'll send Mark Antony to the senate-house,
And he shall say you are not well to-day:
Let me, upon my knee, prevail in this.

CAES.   Mark Antony shall say I am not well,
And, for thy humour, I will stay at home.

Enter DECIUS.

Here's Decius Brutus, he shall tell them so.

DEC.   Caesar, all hail! good morrow, worthy Caesar:
I come to fetch you to the senate-house.

CAES.   And you are come in very happy time,
To bear my greeting to the senators
And tell them that I will not come to-day:
Cannot, is false, and that I dare not, falser:
I will not come to-day: tell them so, Decius.

CAL.   Say he is sick.

CAES.   Shall Caesar send a lie?
Have I in conquest stretch'd mine arm so far,
To be afeard to tell graybeards the truth?
Decius, go tell them Caesar will not come.

DEC.   Most mighty Caesar, let me know some cause,
Lest I be laugh'd at when I tell them so.

CAES.   The cause is in my will: I will not come;
That is enough to satisfy the senate.
But, for your private satisfaction,
Because I love you, I will let you know.
Calpurnia here, my wife, stays me at home:
She dreamt to-night she saw my statue,
Which like a fountain with an hundred spouts
Did run pure blood, and many lusty Romans
Came smiling and did bathe their hands in it:

And these does she apply for warnings and portents
And evils imminent, and on her knee
Hath begg'd that I will stay at home to-day.

DEC.   This dream is all amiss interpreted;
It was a vision fair and fortunate:
Your statue spouting blood in many pipes,
In which so many smiling Romans bathed,
Signifies that from you great Rome shall suck
Reviving blood, and that great men shall press
For tinctures,[3] stains, relics and cognizance.[4]
This by Calpurnia's dream is signified.

CAES.   And this way have you well expounded it.

DEC.   I have, when you have heard what I can say:
And know it now: the senate have concluded
To give this day a crown to mighty Caesar.
If you shall send them word you will not come,
Their minds may change. Besides, it were a mock[5]
Apt to be render'd,[6] for some one to say
"Break up the senate till another time,
When Caesar's wife shall meet with better dreams."
If Caesar hide himself, shall they not whisper
"Lo, Caesar is afraid"?
Pardon me, Caesar, for my dear dear love
To your proceeding[7] bids me tell you this,
And reason to my love is liable.[8]

CAES.   How foolish do your fears seem now, Calpurnia!
I am ashamed I did yield to them.
Give me my robe, for I will go.

Enter PUBLIUS, BRUTUS, LIGARIUS, METELLUS, CASCA, TREBONIUS,
and CINNA.

And look where Publius is come to fetch me.

PUB.   Good morrow, Caesar.

CAES.   Welcome, Publius.
What, Brutus, are you stirr'd so early too?
Good morrow, Casca. Caius Ligarius,

---

3. *tinctures*] handkerchiefs dipped in martyr's blood.
4. *cognizance*] memento.
5. *mock*] sarcasm.
6. *Apt to be render'd*] likely to be offered as a rejoinder.
7. *proceeding*] welfare, advancement.
8. *liable*] subject.

        Caesar was ne'er so much your enemy
        As that same ague which hath made you lean.
        What is't o'clock?
BRU.   Caesar, 't is strucken eight.
CAES.   I thank you for your pains and courtesy.

Enter ANTONY.

        See! Antony, that revels long o' nights,
        Is notwithstanding up. Good morrow, Antony.
ANT.   So to most noble Caesar.
CAES.   Bid them prepare within:
        I am to blame to be thus waited for.
        Now, Cinna: now, Metellus: what, Trebonius!
        I have an hour's talk in store for you;
        Remember that you call on me to-day:
        Be near me, that I may remember you.
TREB. Caesar, I will. [*Aside.*] And so near will I be,
        That your best friends shall wish I had been further.
CAES. Good friends, go in and taste some wine with me;
        And we like friends will straightway go together.
BRU.   [*Aside.*] That every like is not the same, O Caesar,
        The heart of Brutus yearns[9] to think upon!   [*Exeunt.*]

Scene III—A street near the Capitol

Enter ARTEMIDORUS, *reading a paper.*

ART.   "Caesar, beware of Brutus; take heed of Cassius; come not
      near Casca; have an eye to Cinna; trust not Trebonius;
      mark well Metellus Cimber; Decius Brutus loves thee not;
      thou hast wronged Caius Ligarius. There is but one mind
      in all these men, and it is bent against Caesar. If thou beest
      not immortal, look about you: security gives way to[1]
      conspiracy. The mighty gods defend thee!
                    Thy lover,[2] ARTEMIDORUS."

        Here will I stand till Caesar pass along,

9. *yearns*] grieves.

---

1. *security gives way to*] overconfidence opens the road to.
2. *lover*] friend.

And as a suitor will I give him this.
My heart laments that virtue cannot live
Out of the teeth of emulation.[3]
If thou read this, O Caesar, thou mayst live;
If not, the Fates with traitors do contrive.   [*Exit.*]

Scene IV—Another part of the same street, before the house of Brutus

Enter PORTIA *and* LUCIUS.

POR. I prithee, boy, run to the senate-house;
Stay not to answer me, but get thee gone.
Why dost thou stay?

LUC.   To know my errand, madam.

POR. I would have had thee there, and here again,
Ere I can tell thee what thou shouldst do there.
O constancy, be strong upon my side!
Set a huge mountain 'tween my heart and tongue!
I have a man's mind, but a woman's might.
How hard it is for women to keep counsel!
Art thou here yet?

LUC.   Madam, what should I do?
Run to the Capitol, and nothing else?
And so return to you, and nothing else?

POR. Yes, bring me word, boy, if thy lord look well,
For he went sickly forth: and take good note
What Caesar doth, what suitors press to him.
Hark, boy! what noise is that?

LUC. I hear none, madam.

POR.   Prithee, listen well:
I heard a bustling rumour[1] like a fray,
And the wind brings it from the Capitol.

LUC. Sooth, madam, I hear nothing.

Enter the Soothsayer.

POR. Come hither, fellow: which way hast thou been?

3. *emulation*] malicious rivalry.

1. *rumour*] noise.

SOOTH.   At mine own house, good lady.

POR.   What is 't o'clock?

SOOTH.   About the ninth hour, lady.

POR.   Is Caesar yet gone to the Capitol?

SOOTH.   Madam, not yet: I go to take my stand,
To see him pass on to the Capitol.

POR.   Thou hast some suit to Caesar, hast thou not?

SOOTH.   That I have, lady: if it will please Caesar
To be so good to Caesar as to hear me,
I shall beseech him to befriend himself.

POR.   Why, know'st thou any harm's intended towards him?

SOOTH.   None that I know will be, much that I fear may chance.
Good morrow to you. Here the street is narrow:
The throng that follows Caesar at the heels,
Of senators, of praetors, common suitors,
Will crowd a feeble man almost to death:
I'll get me to a place more void and there
Speak to great Caesar as he comes along.   [*Exit.*]

POR.   I must go in. Ay me, how weak a thing
The heart of woman is! O Brutus,
The heavens speed thee in thine enterprise!
Sure, the boy heard me. Brutus hath a suit
That Caesar will not grant. O, I grow faint.
Run, Lucius, and commend me to my lord;
Say I am merry: come to me again,
And bring me word what he doth say to thee. [*Exeunt severally.*]

Act III—Scene I—Rome

BEFORE THE CAPITOL—THE SENATE SITTING ABOVE

A *crowd of people; among them* ARTEMIDORUS *and the* Soothsayer.
Flourish. Enter CAESAR, BRUTUS, CASSIUS, CASCA, DECIUS,
METELLUS, TREBONIUS, CINNA, ANTONY, LEPIDUS, POPILIUS, PUB-
LIUS, *and others.*

CAES.   The ides of March are come.
SOOTH.   Ay, Caesar; but not gone.
ART.   Hail, Caesar! read this schedule.[1]
DEC.   Trebonius doth desire you to o'er-read,
    At your best leisure, this his humble suit.
ART.   O Caesar, read mine first; for mine's a suit
    That touches Caesar nearer: read it, great Caesar.
CAES.   What touches us ourself shall be last served.
ART.   Delay not, Caesar; read it instantly.
CAES.   What, is the fellow mad?
PUB.   Sirrah, give place.
CAS.   What, urge you your petitions in the street?
    Come to the Capitol.

CAESAR *goes up to the Senate-house, the rest following.*

POP.   I wish your enterprise to-day may thrive.
CAS.   What enterprise, Popilius?
POP.   Fare you well. [*Advances to* CAESAR.]
BRU.   What said Popilius Lena?
CAS.   He wish'd to-day our enterprise might thrive.
    I fear our purpose is discovered.
BRU.   Look, how he makes to Caesar: mark him.

1. *schedule*] letter.

35

CAS.   Casca,
　　Be sudden, for we fear prevention.
　　Brutus, what shall be done? If this be known,
　　Cassius or Caesar never shall turn back,
　　For I will slay myself.
BRU.   Cassius, be constant:
　　Popilius Lena speaks not of our purposes;
　　For, look, he smiles, and Caesar doth not change.[2]
CAS.　Trebonius knows his time; for, look you, Brutus,
　　He draws Mark Antony out of the way.
　　　　　　　[*Exeunt* ANTONY *and* TREBONIUS.]
DEC.　Where is Metellus Cimber? Let him go,
　　And presently prefer his suit to Caesar.
BRU.　He is address'd:[3] press near and second him.
CIN.　Casca, you are the first that rears your hand.
CAES.　Are we all ready? What is now amiss
　　That Caesar and his senate must redress?
MET.　Most high, most mighty and most puissant Caesar,
　　Metellus Cimber throws before thy seat
　　An humble heart:—   [*Kneeling.*]
CAES.   I must prevent[4] thee, Cimber.
　　These couchings[5] and these lowly courtesies
　　Might fire the blood of ordinary men,
　　And turn pre-ordinance and first decree
　　Into the law of children. Be not fond,[6]
　　To think that Caesar bears such rebel blood
　　That will be thaw'd from the true quality
　　With that which melteth fools, I mean, sweet words,
　　Low-crooked court'sies and base spaniel-fawning.
　　Thy brother by decree is banished:
　　If thou dost bend and pray and fawn for him,
　　I spurn thee like a cur out of my way.
　　Know, Caesar doth not wrong, nor without cause
　　Will he be satisfied.
MET.　Is there no voice more worthy than my own,
　　To sound more sweetly in great Caesar's ear

2. *change*] change color, turn pale.
3. *address'd*] ready.
4. *prevent*] anticipate.
5. *couchings*] stoopings.
6. *fond*] foolish.

<dl>
<dt></dt>
<dd>For the repealing of my banish'd brother?</dd>
</dl>

BRU.   I kiss thy hand, but not in flattery, Caesar,
      Desiring thee that Publius Cimber may
      Have an immediate freedom of repeal.

CAES.   What, Brutus!

CAS.   Pardon, Caesar; Caesar, pardon:
      As low as to thy foot doth Cassius fall,
      To beg enfranchisement for Publius Cimber.

CAES.   I could be well moved, if I were as you;
      If I could pray to move, prayers would move me:
      But I am constant as the northern star,
      Of whose true-fix'd and resting[7] quality
      There is no fellow in the firmament.
      The skies are painted with unnumber'd sparks;
      They are all fire and every one doth shine;
      But there's but one in all doth hold his place:
      So in the world; 't is furnish'd well with men,
      And men are flesh and blood, and apprehensive:[8]
      Yet in the number I do know but one
      That unassailable holds on his rank,[9]
      Unshaked of motion: and that I am he,
      Let me a little show it, even in this;
      That I was constant Cimber should be banish'd,
      And constant do remain to keep him so.

CIN.   O Caesar,—

CAES.   Hence! wilt thou lift up Olympus?

DEC.   Great Caesar,—

CAES.   Doth not Brutus bootless[10] kneel?

CASCA.   Speak, hands, for me!

             [CASCA *first, then the other* Conspirators *and*
                   MARCUS BRUTUS *stab* CAESAR.]

CAES.   Et tu, Brute? Then fall, Caesar!   [*Dies.*]

CIN.   Liberty! freedom! Tyranny is dead!
      Run hence, proclaim, cry it about the streets.

CAS.   Some to the common pulpits,[11] and cry out
      "Liberty, freedom and enfranchisement!"

BRU.   People, and senators, be not affrighted;

---

7. *resting*] immovable.
8. *apprehensive*] endowed with intelligence.
9. *rank*] position.
10. *bootless*] in vain.
11. *common pulpits*] public rostra.

Fly not; stand still: ambition's debt is paid.

CASCA.   Go to the pulpit, Brutus.

DEC.   And Cassius too.

BRU.   Where's Publius?

CIN.   Here, quite confounded with this mutiny.

MET.   Stand fast together, lest some friend of Caesar's
Should chance—

BRU.   Talk not of standing. Publius, good cheer;
There is no harm intended to your person,
Nor to no Roman else: so tell them, Publius.

CAS.   And leave us, Publius; lest that the people
Rushing on us should do your age some mischief.

BRU.   Do so: and let no man abide[12] this deed
But we the doers.

Re-enter TREBONIUS.

CAS.   Where is Antony?

TRE.   Fled to his house amazed:
Men, wives and children stare, cry out and run
As it were doomsday.

BRU.   Fates, we will know your pleasures:
That we shall die, we know; 't is but the time,
And drawing days out, that men stand upon.[13]

CAS.   Why, he that cuts off twenty years of life
Cuts off so many years of fearing death.

BRU.   Grant that, and then is death a benefit:
So are we Caesar's friends, that have abridged
His time of fearing death. Stoop, Romans, stoop,
And let us bathe our hands in Caesar's blood
Up to the elbows, and besmear our swords:
Then walk we forth, even to the market-place,
And waving our red weapons o'er our heads,
Let's all cry "Peace, freedom and liberty!"

CAS.   Stoop then, and wash. How many ages hence
Shall this our lofty scene be acted over
In states unborn and accents yet unknown!

BRU.   How many times shall Caesar bleed in sport,
That now on Pompey's basis[14] lies along
No worthier than the dust!

12. *abide*] suffer the consequences of.
13. *stand upon*] make of importance.
14. *Pompey's basis*] the base of Pompey's statue.

CAS.   So oft as that shall be,
              So often shall the knot[15] of us be call'd
              The men that gave their country liberty.
DEC.   What, shall we forth?
CAS.   Ay, every man away:
              Brutus shall lead, and we will grace his heels
              With the most boldest and best hearts of Rome.

Enter a Servant.

BRU.   Soft! who comes here? A friend of Antony's.
SERV.   Thus, Brutus, did my master bid me kneel;
              Thus did Mark Antony bid me fall down;
              And, being prostrate, thus he bade me say:
              Brutus is noble, wise, valiant and honest;
              Caesar was mighty, bold, royal and loving:
              Say I love Brutus and I honour him;
              Say I fear'd Caesar, honour'd him and loved him.
              If Brutus will vouchsafe that Antony
              May safely come to him and be resolved[16]
              How Caesar hath deserved to lie in death,
              Mark Antony shall not love Caesar dead
              So well as Brutus living, but will follow
              The fortunes and affairs of noble Brutus
              Thorough[17] the hazards of this untrod state
              With all true faith. So says my master Antony.
BRU.   Thy master is a wise and valiant Roman;
              I never thought him worse.
              Tell him, so please him come unto this place,
              He shall be satisfied and, by my honour,
              Depart untouch'd.
SERV.   I'll fetch him presently.   [*Exit.*]
BRU.   I know that we shall have him well to friend.[18]
CAS.   I wish we may: but yet have I a mind
              That fears him much, and my misgiving still
              Falls shrewdly to the purpose.

Re-enter ANTONY.

BRU.   But here comes Antony. Welcome, Mark Antony.

15. *knot*] band.
16. *resolved*] informed.
17. *Thorough*] through.
18. *to friend*] for a friend.

ANT.   O mighty Caesar! dost thou lie so low?
           Are all thy conquests, glories, triumphs, spoils,
           Shrunk to this little measure? Fare thee well.
           I know not, gentlemen, what you intend,
           Who else must be let blood, who else is rank:[19]
           If I myself, there is no hour so fit
           As Caesar's death's hour, nor no instrument
           Of half that worth as those your swords, made rich
           With the most noble blood of all this world.
           I do beseech ye, if you bear me hard,[20]
           Now, whilst your purpled hands do reek and smoke,
           Fulfil your pleasure. Live[21] a thousand years,
           I shall not find myself so apt to die:
           No place will please me so, no mean of death,
           As here by Caesar, and by you cut off,
           The choice and master spirits of this age.

BRU.   O Antony, beg not your death of us.
           Though now we must appear bloody and cruel,
           As, by our hands and this our present act,
           You see we do; yet see you but our hands
           And this the bleeding business they have done:
           Our hearts you see not; they are pitiful;
           And pity to the general wrong of Rome—
           As fire drives out fire, so pity pity—
           Hath done this deed on Caesar. For your part,
           To you our swords have leaden points, Mark Antony:
           Our arms in strength of malice, and our hearts
           Of brothers' temper, do receive you in
           With all kind love, good thoughts and reverence.

CAS.   Your voice shall be as strong as any man's
           In the disposing of new dignities.[22]

BRU.   Only be patient till we have appeased
           The multitude, beside themselves with fear,
           And then we will deliver you the cause
           Why I, that did love Caesar when I struck him,
           Have thus proceeded.

ANT.   I doubt not of your wisdom.

---

19. *rank*] diseased (hypertrophic).
20. *bear me hard*] harbor a grudge against me.
21. *Live*] should I live.
22. *dignities*] high offices of state.

Sway'd from the point by looking down on Caesar.
Friends am I with you all and love you all,
Upon this hope that you shall give me reasons
Why and wherein Caesar was dangerous.

BRU.   Or else were this a savage spectacle:
Our reasons are so full of good regard[29]
That were you, Antony, the son of Caesar,
You should be satisfied.

ANT.   That's all I seek:
And am moreover suitor that I may
Produce his body to the market-place,[30]
And in the pulpit, as becomes a friend,
Speak in the order of his funeral.

BRU.   You shall, Mark Antony.
CAS.   Brutus, a word with you.
[*Aside to* BRU.] You know not what you do: do not consent
That Antony speak in his funeral:
Know you how much the people may be moved
By that which he will utter?

BRU.   By your pardon:
I will myself into the pulpit first,
And show the reason of our Caesar's death:
What Antony shall speak, I will protest
He speaks by leave and by permission,
And that we are contented Caesar shall
Have all true rites and lawful ceremonies.
It shall advantage more than do us wrong.

CAS.   I know not what may fall; I like it not.
BRU.   Mark Antony, here, take you Caesar's body.
You shall not in your funeral speech blame us,
But speak all good you can devise of Caesar,
And say you do't by our permission;
Else shall you not have any hand at all
About his funeral: and you shall speak
In the same pulpit whereto I am going,
After my speech is ended.

ANT.   Be it so;
I do desire no more.

29. *good regard*] just consideration.
30. *Produce . . . market-place*] carry his body to the Forum.

Let each man render me his bloody hand:
First, Marcus Brutus, will I shake with you;
Next, Caius Cassius, do I take your hand;
Now, Decius Brutus, yours; now yours, Metellus;
Yours, Cinna; and, my valiant Casca, yours;
Though last, not least in love, yours, good Trebonius.
Gentlemen all,—alas, what shall I say?
My credit now stands on such slippery ground,
That one of two bad ways you must conceit me, [23]
Either a coward or a flatterer.
That I did love thee, Caesar, O, 't is true:
If then thy spirit look upon us now,
Shall it not grieve thee dearer than thy death,
To see thy Antony making his peace,
Shaking the bloody fingers of thy foes,
Most noble! in the presence of thy corse?
Had I as many eyes as thou hast wounds,
Weeping as fast as they stream forth thy blood,
It would become me better than to close
In terms of friendship with thine enemies.
Pardon me, Julius! Here wast thou bay'd, brave hart; [24]
Here didst thou fall, and here thy hunters stand,
Sign'd in thy spoil [25] and crimson'd in thy lethe. [26]
O world, thou wast the forest to this hart;
And this, indeed, O world, the heart of thee.
How like a deer strucken by many princes
Dost thou here lie!

CAS.   Mark Antony,—

ANT.   Pardon me, Caius Cassius:
The enemies of Caesar shall say this;
Then, in a friend, it is cold modesty. [27]

CAS.   I blame you not for praising Caesar so;
But what compact mean you to have with us?
Will you be prick'd in number of [28] our friends,
Or shall we on, and not depend on you?

ANT.   Therefore I took your hands, but was indeed

---

23. *conceit me*] think of me.
24. *bay'd, brave hart*] brought to bay, like a deer hunted by hounds.
25. *spoil*] slaughter.
26. *lethe*] death, oblivion.
27. *modesty*] moderation.
28. *prick'd in number of*] enrolled amongst.

BRU. Prepare the body then, and follow us. [*Exeunt all but* ANTONY.]
ANT. O, pardon me, thou bleeding piece of earth,
      That I am meek and gentle with these butchers!
      Thou art the ruins of the noblest man
      That ever lived in the tide of times.
      Woe to the hand that shed this costly blood!
      Over thy wounds now do I prophesy,
      Which like dumb mouths do ope their ruby lips
      To beg the voice and utterance of my tongue,
      A curse shall light upon the limbs of men;
      Domestic fury and fierce civil strife
      Shall cumber all the parts of Italy;
      Blood and destruction shall be so in use,
      And dreadful objects so familiar,
      That mothers shall but smile when they behold
      Their infants quarter'd[31] with the hands of war;
      All pity choked with custom of fell deeds:
      And Caesar's spirit ranging for revenge,
      With Ate[32] by his side come hot from hell,
      Shall in these confines with a monarch's voice
      Cry "Havoc,"[33] and let slip the dogs of war;
      That this foul deed shall smell above the earth
      With carrion men, groaning for burial.

Enter a Servant.

      You serve Octavius Caesar, do you not?
SERV. I do, Mark Antony.
ANT. Caesar did write for him to come to Rome.
SERV. He did receive his letters, and is coming;
      And bid me say to you by word of mouth—
      O Caesar!   [*Seeing the body.*]
ANT. Thy heart is big; get thee apart and weep.
      Passion, I see, is catching, for mine eyes,
      Seeing those beads of sorrow stand in thine,
      Began to water. Is thy master coming?
SERV. He lies to-night within seven leagues of Rome.
ANT. Post back with speed, and tell him what hath chanced:
      Here is a mourning Rome, a dangerous Rome,

31. *quarter'd*] cut to pieces.
32. *Ate*] the goddess of discord in Greek mythology.
33. *"Havoc"*] the signal for pillage and slaughter.

No Rome of safety for Octavius yet;
Hie hence, and tell him so. Yet stay awhile;
Thou shalt not back till I have borne this corse
Into the market-place: there shall I try,
In my oration, how the people take
The cruel issue[34] of these bloody men;
According to the which, thou shalt discourse
To young Octavius of the state of things.
Lend me your hand.   [*Exeunt with* CAESAR'S *body.*]

Scene II—The Forum

Enter BRUTUS *and* CASSIUS, *and a throng of* Citizens.

CITIZENS.   We will be satisfied; let us be satisfied.
BRU.   Then follow me, and give me audience, friends.
        Cassius, go you into the other street,
        And part the numbers.[1]
        Those that will hear me speak, let 'em stay here;
        Those that will follow Cassius, go with him;
        And public reasons shall be rendered
        Of Caesar's death.
FIRST CIT.   ,   I will hear Brutus speak.
SEC. CIT.   I will hear Cassius; and compare their reasons,
        When severally we hear them rendered.
                         [*Exit* CASSIUS, *with some of the* Citizens.
                              BRUTUS *goes into the pulpit.*]
THIRD CIT.   The noble Brutus is ascended: silence!
BRU.   Be patient till the last.
        Romans, countrymen, and lovers![2] hear me for my cause, and be
        silent, that you may hear: believe me for mine honour, and have
        respect to mine honour, that you may believe: censure[3] me in
        your wisdom, and awake your senses, that you may the

34. *issue*] action.
_____
1. *part the numbers*] divide up the crowd.
2. *lovers*] friends.
3. *censure*] judge.

better judge. If there be any in this assembly, any dear friend of Caesar's, to him I say that Brutus' love to Caesar was no less than his. If then that friend demand why Brutus rose against Caesar, this is my answer: not that I loved Caesar less, but that I loved Rome more. Had you rather Caesar were living, and die all slaves, than that Caesar were dead, to live all freemen? As Caesar loved me, I weep for him; as he was fortunate, I rejoice at it; as he was valiant, I honour him; but as he was ambitious, I slew him. There is tears for his love; joy for his fortune; honour for his valour; and death for his ambition. Who is here so base that would be a bondman? If any, speak; for him have I offended. Who is here so rude[4] that would not be a Roman? If any, speak; for him have I offended. Who is here so vile that will not love his country? If any, speak; for him have I offended. I pause for a reply.

ALL.   None, Brutus, none.

BRU.   Then none have I offended. I have done no more to Caesar than you shall do to Brutus. The question of his death is enrolled in the Capitol;[5] his glory not extenuated,[6] wherein he was worthy, nor his offences enforced,[7] for which he suffered death.

Enter ANTONY *and others, with* CAESAR'S *body.*

Here comes his body, mourned by Mark Antony: who, though he had no hand in his death, shall receive the benefit of his dying, a place in the commonwealth; as which of you shall not? With this I depart,—that, as I slew my best lover[8] for the good of Rome, I have the same dagger for myself, when it shall please my country to need my death.

ALL.   Live, Brutus! live, live!

FIRST CIT.   Bring him with triumph home unto his house.

SEC. CIT.   Give him a statue with his ancestors.

THIRD CIT.   Let him be Caesar.

FOURTH CIT.   Caesar's better parts
Shall be crown'd in Brutus.

FIRST CIT.   We'll bring him to his house with shouts and clamours.

BRU.   My countrymen,—

---

4. *rude*] uncivilized.
5. *The question . . . Capitol*] the reasons for his death are recorded in the records of the Senate.
6. *extenuated*] diminished.
7. *enforced*] exaggerated.
8. *lover*] friend.

SEC. CIT.   Peace! silence! Brutus speaks.
FIRST CIT.   Peace, ho!
BRU.   Good countrymen, let me depart alone,
          And, for my sake, stay here with Antony:
          Do grace to Caesar's corpse, and grace his speech
          Tending to Caesar's glories, which Mark Antony
          By our permission is allow'd to make.
          I do entreat you, not a man depart,
          Save I alone, till Antony have spoke.   [*Exit.*]
FIRST CIT.   Stay, ho! and let us hear Mark Antony.
THIRD CIT.   Let him go up into the public chair;⁹
          We'll hear him. Noble Antony, go up.
ANT.   For Brutus' sake, I am beholding¹⁰ to you. [*Goes into the pulpit.*]
FOURTH CIT.   What does he say of Brutus?
THIRD CIT.   He says, for Brutus' sake,
          He finds himself beholding to us all.
FOURTH CIT.   'T were best he speak no harm of Brutus here.
FIRST CIT.   This Caesar was a tyrant.
THIRD CIT.   Nay, that's certain:
          We are blest that Rome is rid of him.
SEC. CIT.   Peace! let us hear what Antony can say.
ANT.   You gentle Romans,—
ALL.   Peace, ho! Let us hear him.
ANT.   Friends, Romans, countrymen, lend me your ears;
          I come to bury Caesar, not to praise him.
          The evil that men do lives after them;
          The good is oft interred with their bones;
          So let it be with Caesar. The noble Brutus
          Hath told you Caesar was ambitious:
          If it were so, it was a grievous fault,
          And grievously hath Caesar answer'd it.¹¹
          Here, under leave of Brutus and the rest,—
          For Brutus is an honourable man;
          So are they all, all honourable men,—
          Come I to speak in Caesar's funeral.
          He was my friend, faithful and just to me:
          But Brutus says he was ambitious;

  9. *the public chair*] the public rostrum (in the Forum).
 10. *beholding*] under obligation.
 11. *answer'd it*] atoned for it.

And Brutus is an honourable man.
He hath brought many captives home to Rome,
Whose ransoms did the general coffers fill:
Did this in Caesar seem ambitious?
When that the poor have cried, Caesar hath wept:
Ambition should be made of sterner stuff:
Yet Brutus says he was ambitious;
And Brutus is an honourable man.
You all did see that on the Lupercal
I thrice presented him a kingly crown,
Which he did thrice refuse: was this ambition?
Yet Brutus says he was ambitious;
And, sure, he is an honourable man.
I speak not to disprove what Brutus spoke,
But here I am to speak what I do know.
You all did love him once, not without cause:
What cause withholds you then to mourn for him?
O judgement! thou art fled to brutish beasts,
And men have lost their reason. Bear with me;
My heart is in the coffin there with Caesar,
And I must pause till it come back to me.

FIRST CIT.   Methinks there is much reason in his sayings.

SEC. CIT.   If thou consider rightly of the matter,
Caesar has had great wrong.

THIRD CIT.   Has he, masters?
I fear there will a worse come in his place.

FOURTH CIT.   Mark'd ye his words? He would not take the crown;
Therefore 't is certain he was not ambitious.

FIRST CIT.   If it be found so, some will dear abide[12] it.

SEC. CIT.   Poor soul! his eyes are red as fire with weeping.

THIRD CIT.   There's not a nobler man in Rome than Antony.

FOURTH CIT.   Now mark him, he begins again to speak.

ANT.   But yesterday the word of Caesar might
Have stood against the world: now lies he there,
And none so poor to do him reverence.
O masters, if I were disposed to stir
Your hearts and minds to mutiny and rage,
I should do Brutus wrong and Cassius wrong,
Who, you all know, are honourable men:
I will not do them wrong; I rather choose

12. *dear abide*] suffer bitterly for.

To wrong the dead, to wrong myself and you,
Than I will wrong such honourable men.
But here's a parchment with the seal of Caesar;
I found it in his closet; 't is his will:
Let but the commons hear this testament—
Which, pardon me, I do not mean to read—
And they would go and kiss dead Caesar's wounds
And dip their napkins[13] in his sacred blood,
Yea, beg a hair of him for memory,
And, dying, mention it within their wills,
Bequeathing it as a rich legacy
Unto their issue.

FOURTH CIT.   We'll hear the will: read it, Mark Antony.

ALL.   The will, the will! we will hear Caesar's will.

ANT.   Have patience, gentle friends, I must not read it;
It is not meet you know how Caesar loved you.
You are not wood, you are not stones, but men;
And, being men, hearing the will of Caesar,
It will inflame you, it will make you mad:
'T is good you know not that you are his heirs;
For if you should, O, what would come of it!

FOURTH CIT.   Read the will; we'll hear it, Antony;
You shall read us the will, Caesar's will.

ANT.   Will you be patient? will you stay a while?
I have o'ershot myself[14] to tell you of it:
I fear I wrong the honourable men
Whose daggers have stabb'd Caesar; I do fear it.

FOURTH CIT.   They were traitors: honourable men!

ALL.   The will! the testament!

SEC. CIT.   They were villains, murderers: the will! read the will.

ANT.   You will compel me then to read the will?
Then make a ring about the corpse of Caesar,
And let me show you him that made the will.
Shall I descend? and will you give me leave?

ALL.   Come down.

SEC. CIT.   Descend.   [*He comes down from the pulpit.*]

THIRD CIT.   You shall have leave.

FOURTH CIT.   A ring; stand round.

FIRST CIT.   Stand from the hearse, stand from the body.

13. *napkins*] handkerchiefs.
14. *o'ershot myself*] gone beyond my intention.

SEC. CIT.   Room for Antony, most noble Antony.

ANT.   Nay, press not so upon me; stand far off.

ALL.   Stand back. Room! Bear back.

ANT.   If you have tears, prepare to shed them now.
    You all do know this mantle: I remember
    The first time ever Caesar put it on;
    'T was on a summer's evening, in his tent,
    That day he overcame the Nervii:[15]
    Look, in this place ran Cassius' dagger through:
    See what a rent the envious[16] Casca made:
    Through this the well-beloved Brutus stabb'd;
    And as he pluck'd his cursed steel away,
    Mark how the blood of Caesar follow'd it,
    As rushing out of doors, to be resolved[17]
    If Brutus so unkindly knock'd, or no:
    For Brutus, as you know, was Caesar's angel:[18]
    Judge, O you gods, how dearly Caesar loved him!
    This was the most unkindest cut of all;
    For when the noble Caesar saw him stab,
    Ingratitude, more strong than traitors' arms,
    Quite vanquish'd him: then burst his mighty heart;
    And, in his mantle muffling up his face,
    Even at the base of Pompey's statue,
    Which all the while ran blood, great Caesar fell.
    O, what a fall was there, my countrymen!
    Then I, and you, and all of us fell down,
    Whilst bloody treason flourish'd over us.
    O, now you weep, and I perceive you feel
    The dint[19] of pity: these are gracious drops.
    Kind souls, what weep you when you but behold
    Our Caesar's vesture wounded? Look you here,
    Here is himself, marr'd, as you see, with[20] traitors.

FIRST CIT.   O piteous spectacle!

SEC. CIT.   O noble Caesar!

THIRD CIT.   O woful day!

FOURTH CIT.   O traitors, villains!

---

15. *Nervii*] a warlike Belgian tribe.
16. *envious*] malicious.
17. *to be resolved*] to ascertain.
18. *angel*] dearest friend.
19. *dint*] stroke or impression.
20. *marr'd . . . with*] defaced by.

FIRST CIT.   O most bloody sight!

SEC. CIT.   We will be revenged.

ALL.   Revenge! About! Seek! Burn! Fire! Kill! Slay! Let not a traitor live!

ANT.   Stay, countrymen.

FIRST CIT.   Peace there! hear the noble Antony.

SEC. CIT.   We'll hear him, we'll follow him, we'll die with him.

ANT.   Good friends, sweet friends, let me not stir you up
To such a sudden flood of mutiny.
They that have done this deed are honourable;
What private griefs[21] they have, alas, I know not,
That made them do it: they are wise and honourable,
And will, no doubt, with reasons answer you.
I come not, friends, to steal away your hearts:
I am no orator, as Brutus is;
But, as you know me all, a plain blunt man,
That love my friend; and that they know full well
That gave me public leave to speak of him:
For I have neither wit,[22] nor words, nor worth,
Action,[23] nor utterance, nor the power of speech,
To stir men's blood: I only speak right on;
I tell you that which you yourselves do know;
Show you sweet Caesar's wounds, poor poor dumb mouths,
And bid them speak for me: but were I Brutus,
And Brutus Antony, there were an Antony
Would ruffle up your spirits, and put a tongue
In every wound of Caesar, that should move
The stones of Rome to rise and mutiny.

ALL.   We'll mutiny.

FIRST CIT.   We'll burn the house of Brutus.

THIRD CIT.   Away, then! come, seek the conspirators.

ANT.   Yet hear me, countrymen; yet hear me speak.

ALL.   Peace, ho! Hear Antony. Most noble Antony!

ANT.   Why, friends, you go to do you know not what:
Wherein hath Caesar thus deserved your loves?
Alas, you know not; I must tell you then:
You have forgot the will I told you of.

ALL.   Most true: the will! Let's stay and hear the will.

ANT.   Here is the will, and under Caesar's seal.

21. *private griefs*] personal grievances.
22. *wit*] intelligence, imagination.
23. *Action*] gesture.

             To every Roman citizen he gives,
             To every several[24] man, seventy-five drachmas.[25]

SEC. CIT.   Most noble Caesar! we'll revenge his death.

THIRD CIT.   O royal Caesar!

ANT.   Hear me with patience.

ALL.   Peace, ho!

ANT.   Moreover, he hath left you all his walks,[26]
             His private arbours and new-planted orchards,
             On this side Tiber; he hath left them you,
             And to your heirs for ever; common pleasures,[27]
             To walk abroad and recreate yourselves.
             Here was a Caesar! when comes such another?

FIRST CIT.   Never, never. Come, away, away!
             We'll burn his body in the holy place,
             And with the brands fire the traitors' houses.
             Take up the body.

SEC. CIT.   Go fetch fire.

THIRD CIT.   Pluck down benches.

FOURTH CIT.   Pluck down forms,[28] windows, any thing.

                                      [Exeunt Citizens *with the body.]*

ANT.   Now let it work. Mischief, thou art afoot,
             Take thou what course thou wilt.

Enter a Servant.

                                     How now, fellow!

SERV.   Sir, Octavius is already come to Rome.

ANT.   Where is he?

SERV.   He and Lepidus are at Caesar's house.

ANT.   And thither will I straight to visit him:
             He comes upon a wish. Fortune is merry,
             And in this mood will give us any thing.

SERV.   I heard him say, Brutus and Cassius
             Are rid[29] like madmen through the gates of Rome.

ANT.   Belike they had some notice of the people,
             How I had moved them. Bring me to Octavius.   *[Exeunt.]*

---

24. *several*] single, individual.
25. *drachmas*] ancient Greek silver coins.
26. *walks*] parks, gardens.
27. *common pleasures*] public pleasure grounds.
28. *forms*] benches.
29. *Are rid*] have ridden.

Scene III—A street

Enter CINNA *the poet.*

CIN. I dreamt to-night that I did feast with Caesar,
And things unluckily charge my fantasy:[1]
I have no will to wander forth of doors,
Yet something leads me forth.

Enter Citizens.

FIRST CIT. What is your name?
SEC. CIT. Whither are you going?
THIRD CIT. Where do you dwell?
FOURTH CIT. Are you a married man or a bachelor?
SEC. CIT. Answer every man directly.
FIRST CIT. Ay, and briefly.
FOURTH CIT. Ay, and wisely.
THIRD CIT. Ay, and truly, you were best.[2]
CIN. What is my name? Whither am I going? Where do I dwell? Am I
a married man or a bachelor? Then, to answer every man directly
and briefly, wisely and truly: wisely I say, I am a bachelor.
SEC. CIT. That's as much as to say, they are fools that marry: you'll bear
me a bang[3] for that, I fear. Proceed; directly.
CIN. Directly, I am going to Caesar's funeral.
FIRST CIT. As a friend or an enemy?
CIN. As a friend.
SEC. CIT. That matter is answered directly.
FOURTH CIT. For your dwelling, briefly.
CIN. Briefly, I dwell by the Capitol.
THIRD CIT. Your name, sir, truly.
CIN. Truly, my name is Cinna.
FIRST CIT. Tear him to pieces; he's a conspirator.
CIN. I am Cinna the poet, I am Cinna the poet.
FOURTH CIT. Tear him for his bad verses, tear him for his bad verses.
CIN. I am not Cinna the conspirator.
FOURTH CIT. It is no matter, his name's Cinna; pluck but his name out
of his heart, and turn him going.
THIRD CIT. Tear him, tear him! Come, brands, ho! fire-brands: to
Brutus', to Cassius'; burn all: some to Decius' house, and some to
Casca's; some to Ligarius': away, go!   [*Exeunt.*]

---

1. *unluckily . . . fantasy*] ominously oppress my imagination.
2. *you were best*] it would be best for you.
3. *bear me a bang*] receive a blow from me.

Act IV—Scene I

A HOUSE IN ROME

ANTONY, OCTAVIUS, *and* LEPIDUS, *seated at a table.*

ANT. These many then shall die; their names are prick'd.[1]

OCT. Your brother too must die; consent you, Lepidus?

LEP. I do consent—

OCT.   Prick him down, Antony.

LEP. Upon condition Publius shall not live,
    Who is your sister's son, Mark Antony.

ANT. He shall not live; look, with a spot[2] I damn him.
    But, Lepidus, go you to Caesar's house;
    Fetch the will hither, and we shall determine
    How to cut off some charge in legacies.

LEP. What, shall I find you here?

OCT. Or here, or at the Capitol.   [*Exit* LEPIDUS.]

ANT. This is a slight unmeritable[3] man,
    Meet to be sent on errands: is it fit,
    The three-fold world[4] divided, he should stand
    One of the three to share it?

OCT.   So you thought him,
    And took his voice who should be prick'd to die
    In our black sentence and proscription.

ANT. Octavius, I have seen more days than you:
    And though we lay these honours on this man,
    To ease ourselves of divers slanderous loads,
    He shall but bear them as the ass bears gold,

1. *prick'd*] put on the list.
2. *spot*] mark (made by a stylus).
3. *slight unmeritable*] insignificant, undeserving.
4. *The three-fold world*] Europe, Asia and Africa.

53

To groan and sweat under the business,
Either led or driven, as we point the way;
And having brought our treasure where we will,
Then take we down his load and turn him off,
Like to the empty ass, to shake his ears
And graze in commons.[5]

OCT.   You may do your will:
But he's a tried and valiant soldier.

ANT. So is my horse, Octavius, and for that
I do appoint him store of provender:
It is a creature that I teach to fight,
To wind,[6] to stop, to run directly on,
His corporal motion govern'd by my spirit.
And, in some taste,[7] is Lepidus but so;
He must be taught, and train'd, and bid go forth;
A barren-spirited fellow; one that feeds
On abjects, orts[8] and imitations,
Which, out of use and staled[9] by other men,
Begin his fashion:[10] do not talk of him
But as a property.[11] And now, Octavius,
Listen great things: Brutus and Cassius
Are levying powers: we must straight make head:[12]
Therefore let our alliance be combined,
Our best friends made, our means stretch'd;
And let us presently go sit in council,
How covert matters may be best disclosed,
And open perils surest answered.

OCT. Let us do so: for we are at the stake,[13]
And bay'd about[14] with many enemies;
And some that smile have in their hearts, I fear,
Millions of mischiefs.   [*Exeunt.*]

---

5. *commons*] public pasture.
6. *wind*] turn.
7. *in some taste*] in some slight degree.
8. *abjects, orts*] forsaken persons and refuse.
9. *staled*] worn-out, rendered obsolete.
10. *Begin his fashion*] form the starting point of his own fashion.
11. *a property*] a theatrical property, a mere tool.
12. *make head*] raise an army.
13. *at the stake*] like a bear tied to a stake in the sport of bearbaiting.
14. *bay'd about*] barked at.

Scene II—Camp near Sardis

BEFORE BRUTUS'S TENT

Drum. Enter BRUTUS, LUCILIUS, LUCIUS, *and* Soldiers; TITINIUS *and*
  PINDARUS *meet them*.

BRU.   Stand, ho!
LUCIL.   Give the word, ho! and stand.
BRU.   What now, Lucilius! is Cassius near?
LUCIL.   He is at hand; and Pindarus is come
        To do you salutation from his master.
BRU.   He greets me well. Your master, Pindarus,
        In his own change,[1] or by ill officers,
        Hath given me some worthy cause to wish
        Things done undone: but if he be at hand,
        I shall be satisfied.
PIN.   I do not doubt
        But that my noble master will appear
        Such as he is, full of regard and honour.
BRU.   He is not doubted. A word, Lucilius,
        How he received you: let me be resolved.
LUCIL.   With courtesy and with respect enough;
        But not with such familiar instances,[2]
        Nor with such free and friendly conference,
        As he hath used of old.
BRU.   Thou hast described
        A hot friend cooling: ever note, Lucilius,
        When love begins to sicken and decay,
        It useth an enforced ceremony.
        There are no tricks in plain and simple faith:
        But hollow[3] men, like horses hot at hand,[4]
        Make gallant show and promise of their mettle;
        But when they should endure the bloody spur,
        They fall their crests[5] and like deceitful jades[6]
        Sink in the trial. Comes his army on?

1. *In his own change*] because of some change of mind on his own part.
2. *familiar instances*] marks of familiarity.
3. *hollow*] insincere.
4. *hot at hand*] spirited when reined in.
5. *fall their crests*] lower their heads.
6. *deceitful jades*] horses not to be trusted.

LUCIL.   They mean this night in Sardis to be quarter'd;
          The greater part, the horse in general,
          Are come with Cassius.   [*Low march within.*]
BRU.   Hark! he is arrived:
          March gently on to meet him.

Enter CASSIUS *and his powers.*

CAS.   Stand, ho!
BRU.   Stand, ho! Speak the word along.
FIRST SOL.   Stand!
SEC. SOL.   Stand!
THIRD SOL.   Stand!
CAS.   Most noble brother, you have done me wrong.
BRU.   Judge me, you gods! wrong I mine enemies?
          And, if not so, how should I wrong a brother?
CAS.   Brutus, this sober form of yours hides wrongs;
          And when you do them—
BRU.   Cassius, be content;
          Speak your griefs[7] softly: I do know you well.
          Before the eyes of both our armies here,
          Which should perceive nothing but love from us,
          Let us not wrangle: bid them move away;
          Then in my tent, Cassius, enlarge your griefs,[8]
          And I will give you audience.
CAS.   Pindarus,
          Bid our commanders lead their charges[9] off
          A little from this ground.
BRU.   Lucilius, do you the like, and let no man
          Come to our tent till we have done our conference.
          Let Lucius and Titinius guard our door.   [*Exeunt.*]

---

7. *griefs*] grievances.
8. *enlarge your griefs*] set out in full your grievances.
9. *charges*] troops.

Scene III—Brutus's tent

Enter BRUTUS *and* CASSIUS.

CAS. That you have wrong'd me doth appear in this:
   You have condemn'd and noted[1] Lucius Pella
   For taking bribes here of the Sardians;
   Wherein my letters, praying on his side,
   Because I knew the man, were slighted off.[2]
BRU. You wrong'd yourself to write in such a case.
CAS. In such a time as this it is not meet
   That every nice[3] offence should bear his comment.[4]
BRU. Let me tell you, Cassius, you yourself
   Are much condemn'd to have an itching palm,
   To sell and mart[5] your offices for gold
   To undeservers.
CAS.   I an itching palm!
   You know that you are Brutus that speaks this,
   Or, by the gods, this speech were else your last.
BRU. The name of Cassius honours this corruption,
   And chastisement doth therefore hide his head.
CAS. Chastisement!
BRU. Remember March, the ides of March remember:
   Did not great Julius bleed for justice' sake?
   What villain touch'd his body, that did stab,
   And not for justice? What, shall one of us,
   That struck the foremost man of all this world
   But for supporting robbers, shall we now
   Contaminate our fingers with base bribes,
   And sell the mighty space of our large honours
   For so much trash as may be grasped thus?
   I had rather be a dog, and bay[6] the moon,
   Than such a Roman.
CAS.   Brutus, bait not me;

---

1. *noted*] disgraced.
2. *slighted off*] disregarded.
3. *nice*] petty.
4. *bear his comment*] be scrutinized.
5. *mart*] trade.
6. *bay*] bark at.

> I'll not endure it: you forget yourself,
> To hedge me in;[7] I am a soldier, I,
> Older in practice, abler than yourself
> To make conditions.[8]

BRU.   Go to; you are not, Cassius.

CAS.   I am.

BRU.   I say you are not.

CAS.   Urge[9] me no more, I shall forget myself;
Have mind upon your health, tempt me no farther.

BRU.   Away, slight[10] man!

CAS.   Is 't possible?

BRU.   Hear me, for I will speak.
Must I give way and room to your rash choler?
Shall I be frighted when a madman stares?

CAS.   O ye gods, ye gods! must I endure all this?

BRU.   All this! ay, more: fret till your proud heart break;
Go show your slaves how choleric you are,
And make your bondmen tremble. Must I budge?
Must I observe[11] you? must I stand and crouch
Under your testy humour? By the gods,
You shall digest the venom of your spleen,
Though it do split you; for, from this day forth,
I'll use you for my mirth, yea, for my laughter,
When you are waspish.

CAS.   Is it come to this?

BRU.   You say you are a better soldier:
Let it appear so; make your vaunting true,
And it shall please me well: for mine own part,
I shall be glad to learn of noble men.

CAS.   You wrong me every way; you wrong me, Brutus;
I said, an elder soldier, not a better:
Did I say, better?

BRU.   If you did, I care not.

CAS.   When Caesar lived, he durst not thus have moved me.

BRU.   Peace, peace! you durst not so have tempted him.

---

7. *hedge me in*] limit my authority.
8. *make conditions*] decide the terms on which offices are to be conferred.
9. *Urge*] exasperate.
10. *slight*] insignificant.
11. *observe*] defer to.

CAS.   I durst not!
BRU.   No.
CAS.   What, durst not tempt him!
BRU.   For your life you durst not.
CAS.   Do not presume too much upon my love;
        I may do that I shall be sorry for.
BRU.   You have done that you should be sorry for.
        There is no terror, Cassius, in your threats;
        For I am arm'd so strong in honesty,
        That they pass by me as the idle wind
        Which I respect not. I did send to you
        For certain sums of gold, which you denied me:
        For I can raise no money by vile means:
        By heaven, I had rather coin my heart,
        And drop my blood for drachmas, than to wring
        From the hard hands of peasants their vile trash
        By any indirection.[12] I did send
        To you for gold to pay my legions,
        Which you denied me: was that done like Cassius?
        Should I have answer'd Caius Cassius so?
        When Marcus Brutus grows so covetous,
        To lock such rascal counters[13] from his friends,
        Be ready, gods, with all your thunderbolts,
        Dash him to pieces!
CAS.   I denied you not.
BRU.   You did.
CAS.   I did not: he was but a fool
        That brought my answer back. Brutus hath rived my heart:
        A friend should bear his friend's infirmities,
        But Brutus makes mine greater than they are.
BRU.   I do not, till you practise them on me.
CAS.   You love me not.
BRU.   I do not like your faults.
CAS.   A friendly eye could never see such faults.
BRU.   A flatterer's would not, though they do appear
        As huge as high Olympus.
CAS.   Come, Antony, and young Octavius, come,
        Revenge yourselves alone on Cassius,
        For Cassius is aweary of the world;

12. *indirection*] dishonesty.
13. *rascal counters*] worthless pieces of money.

Hated by one he loves; braved by his brother;
Check'd like a bondman; all his faults observed,
Set in a note-book, learn'd and conn'd by rote,
To cast into my teeth. O, I could weep
My spirit from mine eyes! There is my dagger,
And here my naked breast; within, a heart
Dearer than Plutus' mine, richer than gold:
If that thou be'st a Roman, take it forth;
I, that denied thee gold, will give my heart:
Strike, as thou didst at Caesar; for I know,
When thou didst hate him worst, thou lovedst him better
Than ever thou lovedst Cassius.

BRU.   Sheathe your dagger:
Be angry when you will, it shall have scope;
Do what you will, dishonour shall be humour.[14]
O Cassius, you are yoked with a lamb,
That carries anger as the flint bears fire,
Who, much enforced, shows a hasty spark
And straight is cold again.

CAS.   Hath Cassius lived
To be but mirth and laughter to his Brutus,
When grief and blood ill-temper'd vexeth him?

BRU.   When I spoke that, I was ill-temper'd too.

CAS.   Do you confess so much? Give me your hand.

BRU.   And my heart too.

CAS.   O Brutus!

BRU.   What's the matter?

CAS.   Have not you love enough to bear with me,
When that rash humour which my mother gave me
Makes me forgetful?

BRU.   Yes, Cassius, and from henceforth,
When you are over-earnest with your Brutus,
He'll think your mother chides, and leave you so.

POET.   [*Within.*] Let me go in to see the generals;
There is some grudge between 'em; 't is not meet
They be alone.

LUCIL.   [*Within.*] You shall not come to them.

POET.   [*Within.*] Nothing but death shall stay me.

Enter Poet, *followed by* LUCILIUS, TITINIUS, *and* LUCIUS.

14. *Do . . . humour*] Whatever dishonorable thing you may do, I will set it down to the
    whim or caprice of the moment.

CAS.   How now! what's the matter?
POET.   For shame, you generals! what do you mean?
        Love, and be friends, as two such men should be;
        For I have seen more years, I'm sure, than ye.
CAS.   Ha, ha! how vilely doth this cynic[15] rhyme!
BRU.   Get you hence, sirrah; saucy fellow, hence!
CAS.   Bear with him, Brutus; 't is his fashion.
BRU.   I'll know his humour when he knows his time:
        What should the wars do with these jigging[16] fools?
        Companion,[17] hence!
CAS.   Away, away, be gone!   [Exit Poet.]
BRU.   Lucilius and Titinius, bid the commanders
        Prepare to lodge their companies to-night.
CAS.   And come yourselves, and bring Messala with you
        Immediately to us.   [Exeunt LUCILIUS and TITINIUS.]
BRU.   Lucius, a bowl of wine!   [Exit LUCIUS.]
CAS.   I did not think you could have been so angry.
BRU.   O Cassius, I am sick of many griefs.
CAS.   Of your philosophy you make no use,
        If you give place to accidental evils.
BRU.   No man bears sorrow better: Portia is dead.
CAS.   Ha! Portia!
BRU.   She is dead.
CAS.   How 'scaped I killing when I cross'd you so?
        O insupportable and touching loss!
        Upon what sickness?
BRU.   Impatient of my absence,
        And grief that young Octavius with Mark Antony
        Have made themselves so strong: for with her death
        That tidings came: with this she fell distract,
        And, her attendants absent, swallow'd fire.[18]
CAS.   And died so?
BRU.   Even so.
CAS.   O ye immortal gods!

Re-enter LUCIUS, *with wine and taper.*

BRU.   Speak no more of her. Give me a bowl of wine.

15. *cynic*] uncouth man.
16. *jigging*] often used of doggerel rhyming, as well as of dancing.
17. *Companion*] fellow (used contemptuously).
18. *swallow'd fire*] According to Plutarch, Portia put burning coals in her mouth, and
    then kept her lips closed until she choked.

In this I bury all unkindness, Cassius.   [*Drinks.*]

CAS. My heart is thirsty for that noble pledge.
      Fill, Lucius, till the wine o'erswell the cup;
      I cannot drink too much of Brutus' love.   [*Drinks.*]

BRU. Come in, Titinius!   [*Exit* LUCIUS.]

Re-enter TITINIUS, *with* MESSALA.

                 Welcome, good Messala.
      Now sit we close about this taper here,
      And call in question our necessities.

CAS. Portia, art thou gone?

BRU.   No more, I pray you.
      Messala, I have here received letters,
      That young Octavius and Mark Antony
      Come down upon us with a mighty power,
      Bending their expedition toward Philippi.

MES. Myself have letters of the selfsame tenour.

BRU. With what addition?

MES. That by proscription and bills of outlawry
      Octavius, Antony and Lepidus,
      Have put to death an hundred senators.

BRU. Therein our letters do not well agree;
      Mine speak of seventy senators that died
      By their proscriptions, Cicero being one.

CAS. Cicero one!

MES.   Cicero is dead,
      And by that order of proscription.
      Had you your letters from your wife, my lord?

BRU. No, Messala.

MES. Nor nothing in your letters writ of her?

BRU. Nothing, Messala.

MES.   That, methinks, is strange.

BRU. Why ask you? hear you ought of her in yours?

MES. No, my lord.

BRU. Now, as you are a Roman, tell me true.

MES. Then like a Roman bear the truth I tell:
      For certain she is dead, and by strange manner.

BRU. Why, farewell, Portia. We must die, Messala:
      With meditating that she must die once
      I have the patience to endure it now.

MES. Even so great men great losses should endure.

CAS. I have as much of this in art[19] as you,
     But yet my nature could not bear it so.
BRU. Well, to our work alive. What do you think
     Of marching to Philippi presently?
CAS. I do not think it good.
BRU.   Your reason?
CAS.   This it is:
     'T is better that the enemy seek us:
     So shall he waste his means, weary his soldiers,
     Doing himself offence;[20] whilst we lying still
     Are full of rest, defence and nimbleness.
BRU. Good reasons must of force give place to better.
     The people 'twixt Philippi and this ground
     Do stand but in a forced affection,
     For they have grudged us contribution:
     The enemy, marching along by them,
     By them shall make a fuller number up,
     Come on refresh'd, new-added[21] and encouraged;
     From which advantage shall we cut him off
     If at Philippi we do face him there,
     These people at our back.
CAS.   Hear me, good brother.
BRU. Under your pardon. You must note beside
     That we have tried the utmost of our friends,
     Our legions are brim-full, our cause is ripe:
     The enemy increaseth every day;
     We, at the height, are ready to decline.
     There is a tide in the affairs of men
     Which taken at the flood leads on to fortune;
     Omitted,[22] all the voyage of their life
     Is bound in shallows and in miseries.
     On such a full sea are we now afloat,
     And we must take the current when it serves,
     Or lose our ventures.
CAS.   Then, with your will, go on;
     We'll along ourselves and meet them at Philippi.
BRU. The deep of night is crept upon our talk,

19. *in art*] in theory.
20. *offence*] harm, injury.
21. *new-added*] reinforced.
22. *Omitted*] neglected.

And nature must obey necessity;
Which we will niggard[23] with a little rest.
There is no more to say?

CAS.   No more. Good night:
Early to-morrow will we rise and hence.

BRU.   Lucius! [*Re-enter* LUCIUS.] My gown.   [*Exit* LUCIUS.]
                              Farewell, good Messala:
Good night, Titinius: noble, noble Cassius,
Good night, and good repose.

CAS.   O my dear brother!
This was an ill beginning of the night:
Never come such division 'tween our souls!
Let it not, Brutus.

BRU.   Every thing is well.

CAS.   Good night, my lord.

BRU.   Good night, good brother.

TIT. MES.   Good night, Lord Brutus.

BRU.   Farewell, every one.
                            [*Exeunt all but* BRUTUS.]

Re-enter LUCIUS, *with the gown.*

Give me the gown. Where is thy instrument?

LUC.   Here in the tent.

BRU.   What, thou speak'st drowsily?
Poor knave,[24] I blame thee not; thou art o'er-watch'd.[25]
Call Claudius and some other of my men;
I'll have them sleep on cushions in my tent.

LUC.   Varro and Claudius!

Enter VARRO *and* CLAUDIUS.

VAR.   Calls my lord?

BRU.   I pray you, sirs, lie in my tent and sleep;
It may be I shall raise you by and by
On business to my brother Cassius.

VAR.   So please you, we will stand and watch your pleasure.

BRU.   I will not have it so: lie down, good sirs;
It may be I shall otherwise bethink me.
Look, Lucius, here's the book I sought for so;

---

23. *niggard*] satisfy sparingly.
24. *knave*] lad.
25. *o'er-watch'd*] wearied by lack of sleep.

	I put it in the pocket of my gown. [VAR. *and* CLAU. *lie down.*]
LUC.	I was sure your lordship did not give it me.
BRU.	Bear with me, good boy, I am much forgetful.
	Canst thou hold up thy heavy eyes a while,
	And touch thy instrument a strain or two?
LUC.	Ay, my lord, an 't please you.
BRU.	It does, my boy:
	I trouble thee too much, but thou art willing.
LUC.	It is my duty, sir.
BRU.	I should not urge thy duty past thy might;
	I know young bloods look for a time of rest.
LUC.	I have slept, my lord, already.
BRU.	It was well done; and thou shalt sleep again;
	I will not hold thee long: if I do live,
	I will be good to thee. [*Music, and a song.*]
	This is a sleepy tune. O murderous slumber,
	Lay'st thou thy leaden mace[26] upon my boy,
	That plays thee music? Gentle knave, good night;
	I will not do thee so much wrong to wake thee:
	If thou dost nod, thou break'st thy instrument;
	I'll take it from thee; and, good boy, good night.
	Let me see, let me see; is not the leaf turn'd down
	Where I left reading? Here it is, I think. [*Sits down.*]

Enter the Ghost of CAESAR.

	How ill this taper burns! Ha! who comes here?
	I think it is the weakness of mine eyes
	That shapes this monstrous apparition.
	It comes upon me. Art thou any thing?
	Art thou some god, some angel, or some devil,
	That makest my blood cold, and my hair to stare?[27]
	Speak to me what thou art.
GHOST.	Thy evil spirit, Brutus.
BRU.	Why comest thou?
GHOST.	To tell thee thou shalt see me at Philippi.
BRU.	Well; then I shall see thee again?
GHOST.	Ay, at Philippi.
BRU.	Why, I will see thee at Philippi then. [*Exit Ghost.*]
	Now I have taken heart thou vanishest.

26. *mace*] scepter.
27. *stare*] stand on end.

	Ill spirit, I would hold more talk with thee.
	Boy, Lucius! Varro! Claudius! Sirs awake!
	Claudius!
LUC.	The strings, my lord, are false.
BRU.	He thinks he still is at his instrument.
	Lucius, awake!
LUC.	My lord?
BRU.	Didst thou dream, Lucius, that thou so criedst out?
LUC.	My lord, I do not know that I did cry.
BRU.	Yes, that thou didst: didst thou see any thing?
LUC.	Nothing, my lord.
BRU.	Sleep again, Lucius. Sirrah Claudius!
	[*To* VAR.] Fellow thou, awake!
VAR.	My lord?
CLAU.	My lord?
BRU.	Why did you so cry out, sirs, in your sleep?
VAR. CLAU.	Did we, my lord?
BRU.	Ay: saw you any thing?
VAR.	No, my lord, I saw nothing.
CLAU.	Nor I, my lord.
BRU.	Go and commend me to my brother Cassius;
	Bid him set on his powers betimes before,
	And we will follow.
VAR. CLAU.	It shall be done, my lord. [*Exeunt.*]

Act V—Scene I

THE PLAINS OF PHILIPPI

Enter OCTAVIUS, ANTONY, *and their* Army.

OCT. Now, Antony, our hopes are answered:
 You said the enemy would not come down,
 But keep the hills and upper regions;
 It proves not so: their battles[1] are at hand;
 They mean to warn[2] us at Philippi here,
 Answering before we do demand of them.

ANT. Tut, I am in their bosoms, and I know
 Wherefore they do it: they could be content
 To visit other places; and come down
 With fearful bravery,[3] thinking by this face
 To fasten in our thoughts that they have courage;
 But 't is not so.

Enter a Messenger.

MESS.   Prepare you, generals:
 The enemy comes on in gallant show;
 Their bloody sign of battle is hung out,
 And something to be done immediately.

ANT. Octavius, lead your battle softly on,
 Upon the left hand of the even field.

OCT. Upon the right hand I; keep thou the left.

ANT. Why do you cross[4] me in this exigent?[5]

1. *battles*] battalions.
2. *warn*] challenge.
3. *fearful bravery*] a timid show of courage.
4. *cross*] contradict.
5. *exigent*] emergency.

67

Oct.   I do not cross you; but I will do so.[6]   [*March.*]

Drum. Enter Brutus, Cassius, *and their* Army; Lucilius, Titinius, Messala, *and others.*

Bru.   They stand, and would have parley.

Cas.   Stand fast, Titinius: we must out and talk.

Oct.   Mark Antony, shall we give sign of battle?

Ant.   No, Caesar, we will answer on their charge.[7]
       Make forth; the generals would have some words.

Oct.   Stir not until the signal.

Bru.   Words before blows: is it so, countrymen?

Oct.   Not that we love words better, as you do.

Bru.   Good words are better than bad strokes, Octavius.

Ant.   In your bad strokes, Brutus, you give good words:
       Witness the hole you made in Caesar's heart,
       Crying "Long live! hail, Caesar!"

Cas.   Antony,
       The posture[8] of your blows are yet unknown;
       But for your words, they rob the Hybla bees,[9]
       And leave them honeyless.

Ant.   Not stingless too.

Bru.   O, yes, and soundless too;
       For you have stol'n their buzzing, Antony,
       And very wisely threat before you sting.

Ant.   Villains, you did not so, when your vile daggers
       Hack'd one another in the sides of Caesar:
       You show'd your teeth like apes, and fawn'd like hounds,
       And bow'd like bondmen, kissing Caesar's feet;
       Whilst damned Casca, like a cur, behind
       Struck Caesar on the neck. O you flatterers!

Cas.   Flatterers! Now, Brutus, thank yourself:
       This tongue had not offended so to-day,
       If Cassius might have ruled.

Oct.   Come, come, the cause: if arguing make us sweat,
       The proof of it will turn to redder drops.
       Look;

---

6. *I will do so*] I will have my way.

7. *answer on their charge*] meet them when they charge.

8. *posture*] quality.

9. *the Hybla bees*] Hybla was a town in Sicily celebrated by classical poets for the sweetness of its honey.

I draw a sword against conspirators;
When think you that the sword goes up again?
Never, till Caesar's three and thirty wounds
Be well avenged, or till another Caesar
Have added slaughter to the sword of traitors.

BRU. Caesar, thou canst not die by traitors' hands,
Unless thou bring'st them with thee.

OCT.   So I hope;
I was not born to die on Brutus' sword.

BRU. O, if thou wert the noblest of thy strain,
Young man, thou couldst not die more honourable.

CAS. A peevish schoolboy, worthless of such honour,
Join'd with a masker and a reveller!

ANT. Old Cassius still!

OCT.   Come, Antony; away!
Defiance, traitors, hurl we in your teeth;
If you dare fight to-day, come to the field:
If not, when you have stomachs.[10]

                [*Exeunt* OCTAVIUS, ANTONY, *and their* Army.]

CAS. Why, now, blow wind, swell billow, and swim bark!
The storm is up, and all is on the hazard.

BRU. Ho, Lucilius! hark, a word with you.

LUCIL.   [*Standing forth.*] My lord?
                [BRUTUS *and* LUCILIUS *converse apart.*]

CAS. Messala!

MES. [*Standing forth.*] What says my general?

CAS.   Messala,
This is my birth-day; as[11] this very day
Was Cassius born. Give me thy hand, Messala:
Be thou my witness that, against my will,
As Pompey was, am I compell'd to set
Upon one battle all our liberties.
You know that I held Epicurus[12] strong,
And his opinion: now I change my mind,
And partly credit things that do presage.
Coming from Sardis, on our former[13] ensign
Two mighty eagles fell, and there they perch'd,

10. *stomachs*] inclination.
11. *as*] on.
12. *Epicurus*] the Greek philosopher, who rejected the Stoics' belief in omens.
13. *former*] foremost.

Gorging and feeding from our soldiers' hands;
Who to Philippi here consorted[14] us:
This morning are they fled away and gone;
And in their steads do ravens, crows and kites
Fly o'er our heads and downward look on us,
As we were sickly prey: their shadows seem
A canopy most fatal, under which
Our army lies, ready to give up the ghost.

MES.   Believe not so.

CAS.   I but believe it partly,
For I am fresh of spirit and resolved
To meet all perils very constantly.

BRU.   Even so, Lucilius.

CAS.   Now, most noble Brutus,
The gods to-day stand friendly, that we may,
Lovers[15] in peace, lead on our days to age!
But, since the affairs of men rest still incertain,
Let's reason with[16] the worst that may befall.
If we do lose this battle, then is this
The very last time we shall speak together:
What are you then determined to do?

BRU.   Even by the rule of that philosophy
By which I did blame Cato[17] for the death
Which he did give himself: I know not how,
But I do find it cowardly and vile,
For fear of what might fall, so to prevent
The time of life:[18] arming myself with patience
To stay[19] the providence of some high powers
That govern us below.

CAS.   Then, if we lose this battle,
You are contented to be led in triumph
Thorough the streets of Rome?

BRU.   No, Cassius, no: think not, thou noble Roman,
That ever Brutus will go bound to Rome;

---

14. *consorted*] accompanied.
15. *Lovers*] friends.
16. *reason with*] talk of.
17. *Cato*] the Stoic philosopher, who loyally supported Pompey. After the defeat by Caesar of Pompey's friends at the battle of Thapsus, 46 B.C., Cato committed suicide at Utica, in Africa.
18. *prevent The time of life*] anticipate the normal close of life.
19. *stay*] await.

He bears too great a mind. But this same day
Must end that work the ides of March begun;
And whether we shall meet again I know not.
Therefore our everlasting farewell take.
For ever, and for ever, farewell, Cassius!
If we do meet again, why, we shall smile;
If not, why then this parting was well made.

CAS.   For ever and for ever farewell, Brutus!
If we do meet again, we'll smile indeed;
If not, 't is true this parting was well made.

BRU.   Why then, lead on. O, that a man might know
The end of this day's business ere it come!
But it sufficeth that the day will end,
And then the end is known. Come, ho! away!   [*Exeunt.*]

Scene II—The field of battle

Alarum. Enter BRUTUS *and* MESSALA.

BRU.   Ride, ride, Messala, ride, and give these bills[1]
Unto the legions on the other side: [*Loud alarum.*]
Let them set on at once; for I perceive
But cold demeanour in Octavius' wing,
And sudden push gives them the overthrow.
Ride, ride, Messala: let them all come down.   [*Exeunt.*]

Scene III—Another part of the field

Alarums. Enter CASSIUS *and* TITINIUS.

CAS.   O, look, Titinius, look, the villains fly!
Myself have to mine own turn'd enemy:

1. *bills*] orders.

This ensign[1] here of mine was turning back;
I slew the coward, and did take it from him.

TIT. O Cassius, Brutus gave the word too early;
Who, having some advantage on Octavius,
Took it too eagerly: his soldiers fell to spoil,
Whilst we by Antony are all enclosed.

Enter PINDARUS.

PIN. Fly further off, my lord, fly further off;
Mark Antony is in your tents, my lord:
Fly, therefore, noble Cassius, fly far off.

CAS. This hill is far enough. Look, look, Titinius;
Are those my tents where I perceive the fire?

TIT. They are, my lord.

CAS.   Titinius, if thou lovest me,
Mount thou my horse and hide thy spurs in him,
Till he have brought thee up to yonder troops
And here again; that I may rest assured
Whether yond troops are friend or enemy.

TIT. I will be here again, even with a thought.[2]   [*Exit.*]

CAS. Go, Pindarus, get higher on that hill;
My sight was ever thick;[3] regard Titinius,
And tell me what thou notest about the field.

                                      [*Pindarus ascends the hill.*]

This day I breathed first: time is come round,
And where I did begin, there shall I end;
My life is run his compass. Sirrah, what news?

PIN. [*Above.*] O my lord!

CAS. What news?

PIN. [*Above.*] Titinius is enclosed round about
With horsemen, that make to him on the spur;
Yet he spurs on. Now they are almost on him.
Now, Titinius! Now some light.[4] O, he lights too.
He's ta'en. [*Shout.*] And, hark! they shout for joy.

CAS. Come down; behold no more.
O, coward that I am, to live so long,
To see my best friend ta'en before my face!

1. *ensign*] standard-bearer.
2. *even with a thought*] quick as thought.
3. *thick*] dim.
4. *light*] dismount.

PINDARUS *descends.*

> Come hither, sirrah:
> In Parthia did I take thee prisoner;
> And then I swore thee, saving of thy life,
> That whatsoever I did bid thee do,
> Thou shouldst attempt it. Come now, keep thine oath;
> Now be a freeman; and with this good sword,
> That ran through Caesar's bowels, search this bosom.
> Stand not to answer: here, take thou the hilts;⁵
> And when my face is covered, as 't is now,
> Guide thou the sword. [*Pindarus stabs him.*] Caesar, thou art
>   revenged,
> Even with this sword that kill'd thee.   [*Dies.*]

PIN.   So, I am free; yet would not so have been,
> Durst I have done my will. O Cassius!
> Far from this country Pindarus shall run,
> Where never Roman shall take note of him.   [*Exit.*]

Re-enter TITINIUS *with* MESSALA.

MES.   It is but change,⁶ Titinius; for Octavius
> Is overthrown by noble Brutus' power,
> As Cassius' legions are by Antony.

TIT.   These tidings will well comfort Cassius.

MES.   Where did you leave him?

TIT.   All disconsolate,
> With Pindarus his bondman, on this hill.

MES.   Is not that he that lies upon the ground?

TIT.   He lies not like the living. O my heart!

MES.   Is not that he?

TIT.   No, this was he, Messala,
> But Cassius is no more. O setting sun,
> As in thy red rays thou dost sink to night,
> So in his red blood Cassius' day is set,
> The sun of Rome is set! Our day is gone;
> Clouds, dews and dangers come; our deeds are done!
> Mistrust of my success hath done this deed.

MES.   Mistrust of good success⁷ hath done this deed.
> O hateful error, melancholy's child,

---

5. *hilts*] handle.
6. *change*] i.e., of fortune.
7. *Mistrust of good success*] doubt of a favorable result.

      Why dost thou show to the apt[8] thoughts of men
      The things that are not? O error, soon conceived,
      Thou never comest unto a happy birth,
      But kill'st the mother that engender'd thee!
TIT.   What, Pindarus! where art thou, Pindarus?
MES.   Seek him, Titinius, whilst I go to meet
      The noble Brutus, thrusting this report
      Into his ears: I may say "thrusting" it,
      For piercing steel and darts envenomed
      Shall be as welcome to the ears of Brutus
      As tidings of this sight.
TIT.   Hie you, Messala,
      And I will seek for Pindarus the while.   [*Exit* MESSALA.]
      Why didst thou send me forth, brave Cassius?
      Did I not meet thy friends? and did not they
      Put on my brows this wreath of victory,
      And bid me give it thee? Didst thou not hear their shouts?
      Alas, thou hast misconstrued every thing!
      But, hold thee, take this garland on thy brow;
      Thy Brutus bid me give it thee, and I
      Will do his bidding. Brutus, come apace,
      And see how I regarded Caius Cassius.
      By your leave, gods: this is a Roman's part:
      Come, Cassius' sword, and find Titinius' heart. [*Kills himself.*]

Alarum. Re-enter MESSALA, *with* BRUTUS, *young* CATO, *and others.*

BRU.   Where, where, Messala, doth his body lie?
MES.   Lo, yonder, and Titinius mourning it.
BRU.   Titinius' face is upward.
CATO.   He is slain.
BRU.   O Julius Caesar, thou art mighty yet!
      Thy spirit walks abroad, and turns our swords
      In our own proper entrails.   [*Low alarums.*]
CATO.   Brave Titinius!
      Look, whether he have not crown'd dead Cassius!
BRU.   Are yet two Romans living such as these?
      The last of all the Romans, fare thee well!
      It is impossible that ever Rome
      Should breed thy fellow. Friends, I owe moe tears
      To this dead man than you shall see me pay.

8. *apt*] impressionable.

I shall find time, Cassius, I shall find time.
Come therefore, and to Thasos[9] send his body:
His funerals shall not be in our camp,
Lest it discomfort[10] us. Lucilius, come,
And come, young Cato: let us to the field.
Labeo and Flavius, set our battles on.[11]
'T is three o'clock; and, Romans, yet ere night
We shall try fortune in a second fight.   [*Exeunt.*]

Scene IV—Another part of the field

Alarum. Enter, fighting, Soldiers *of both armies; then* BRUTUS, *young*
CATO, LUCILIUS, *and others.*

BRU.   Yet, countrymen, O, yet hold up your heads!
CATO.   What bastard doth not? Who will go with me?
        I will proclaim my name about the field.
        I am the son of Marcus Cato, ho!
        A foe to tyrants, and my country's friend;
        I am the son of Marcus Cato, ho!
BRU.   And I am Brutus, Marcus Brutus, I;
        Brutus, my country's friend; know me for Brutus!   [*Exit.*]
LUCIL.   O young and noble Cato, art thou down?
        Why, now thou diest as bravely as Titinius,
        And mayst be honour'd, being Cato's son.
FIRST SOLD.   Yield, or thou diest.
LUCIL.   Only I yield to die:
        [*Offering money.*] There is so much that thou wilt kill me straight;
        Kill Brutus, and be honour'd in his death.
FIRST SOLD.   We must not. A noble prisoner!
SEC. SOLD.   Room, ho! Tell Antony, Brutus is ta'en.
FIRST SOLD.   I'll tell the news. Here comes the general.

Enter ANTONY.

        Brutus is ta'en, Brutus is ta'en, my lord.

9. *Thasos*] an island in the Aegean Sea, not far from the battlefield of Philippi.
10. *discomfort*] discourage.
11. *set our battles on*] advance our army.

ANT.   Where is he?

LUCIL.   Safe, Antony; Brutus is safe enough:
            I dare assure thee that no enemy
            Shall ever take alive the noble Brutus:
            The gods defend him from so great a shame!
            When you do find him, or alive or dead,
            He will be found like Brutus, like himself.

ANT.   This is not Brutus, friend, but, I assure you,
            A prize no less in worth: keep this man safe,
            Give him all kindness: I had rather have
            Such men my friends than enemies. Go on,
            And see whether Brutus be alive or dead,
            And bring us word unto Octavius' tent
            How every thing is chanced.   [*Exeunt.*]

Scene V—Another part of the field

Enter BRUTUS, DARDANIUS, CLITUS, STRATO, *and* VOLUMNIUS.

BRU.   Come, poor remains of friends, rest on this rock.

CLI.   Statilius show'd the torch-light,[1] but, my lord,
            He came not back: he is or ta'en or slain.

BRU.   Sit thee down, Clitus: slaying is the word;
            It is a deed in fashion. Hark thee, Clitus.   [*Whispering.*]

CLI.   What, I, my lord? No, not for all the world.

BRU.   Peace then, no words.

CLI.   I'll rather kill myself.

BRU.   Hark thee, Dardanius.   [*Whispering.*]

DAR.   Shall I do such a deed?

CLI.   O Dardanius!

DAR.   O Clitus!

CLI.   What ill request did Brutus make to thee?

DAR.   To kill him, Clitus. Look, he meditates.

CLI.   Now is that noble vessel full of grief,
            That it runs over even at his eyes.

BRU.   Come hither, good Volumnius; list a word.

VOL.   What says my lord?

BRU.   Why, this, Volumnius:

---

1. *show'd the torch-light*] signaled.

The ghost of Caesar hath appear'd to me
Two several times by night; at Sardis once,
And this last night here in Philippi fields:
I know my hour is come.

VOL.   Not so, my lord.
BRU. Nay, I am sure it is, Volumnius.
Thou seest the world, Volumnius, how it goes;
Our enemies have beat us to the pit:[2]   [*Low alarums.*]
It is more worthy to leap in ourselves
Than tarry till they push us. Good Volumnius,
Thou know'st that we two went to school together:
Even for that our love of old, I prithee,
Hold thou my sword-hilts, whilst I run on it.

VOL. That's not an office for a friend, my lord.   [*Alarum still.*]
CLI. Fly, fly, my lord; there is no tarrying here.
BRU. Farewell to you; and you; and you, Volumnius.
Strato, thou hast been all this while asleep;
Farewell to thee too, Strato. Countrymen,
My heart doth joy that yet in all my life
I found no man but he was true to me.
I shall have glory by this losing day,
More than Octavius and Mark Antony
By this vile conquest shall attain unto.
So, fare you well at once; for Brutus' tongue
Hath almost ended his life's history:
Night hangs upon mine eyes; my bones would rest,
That have but labour'd to attain this hour.
                [*Alarum. Cry within,* "Fly, fly, fly!"]

CLI. Fly, my lord, fly.
BRU.   Hence! I will follow.
                [*Exeunt* CLITUS, DARDANIUS, *and* VOLUMNIUS.]
I prithee, Strato, stay thou by thy lord:
Thou art a fellow of a good respect;[3]
Thy life hath had some smatch[4] of honour in it:
Hold then my sword, and turn away thy face,
While I do run upon it. Wilt thou, Strato?
STRA. Give me your hand first: fare you well, my lord.

---

2. *pit*] animal trap, grave.
3. *respect*] reputation.
4. *smatch*] smack, tinge.

BRU.   Farewell, good Strato. [*Runs on his sword.*] Caesar, now be still:
         I kill'd not thee with half so good a will.   [*Dies.*]

Alarum. Retreat. Enter OCTAVIUS, ANTONY, MESSALA, LUCILIUS, *and
   the* Army.

OCT.   What man is that?
MES.   My master's man. Strato, where is thy master?
STRA.   Free from the bondage you are in, Messala:
         The conquerors can but make a fire of him;
         For Brutus only overcame himself,
         And no man else hath honour by his death.
LUCIL.   So Brutus should be found. I thank thee, Brutus,
         That thou hast proved Lucilius' saying true.
OCT.   All that served Brutus, I will entertain them.[5]
         Fellow, wilt thou bestow thy time with me?
STRA.   Ay, if Messala will prefer[6] me to you.
OCT.   Do so, good Messala.
MES.   How died my master, Strato?
STRA.   I held the sword, and he did run on it.
MES.   Octavius, then take him to follow thee,
         That did the latest service to my master.
ANT.   This was the noblest Roman of them all:
         All the conspirators, save only he,
         Did that they did in envy of great Caesar;
         He only, in a general honest thought[7]
         And common good to all, made one of them.
         His life was gentle, and the elements
         So mix'd in him that Nature might stand up
         And say to all the world "This was a man!"
OCT.   According to his virtue let us use him,
         With all respect and rites of burial.
         Within my tent his bones to-night shall lie,
         Most like a soldier, order'd honourably.
         So call the field to rest, and let's away,
         To part[8] the glories of this happy day.   [*Exeunt.*]

5. *entertain them*] take them into my service.
6. *prefer*] recommend.
7. *general honest thought*] an honest concern for the public good.
8. *part*] distribute.

Study Guide

Text by

Joseph E. Scalia

(M.A., Brooklyn College)

Department of English
Hicksville High School
Hicksville, New York

Contents

**Each scene includes List of Characters,
Summary, Analysis, Study Questions and
Answers, and Suggested Essay Topics.**

SECTION ONE

Introduction

The Life and Work of William Shakespeare

William Shakespeare (1564–1616) is perhaps the most widely read English poet and dramatist in the world. His plays and poems have been translated into every major language, and his popularity, nearly 400 years after his death, is greater now than it was in his own lifetime. Yet very little is known about his personal and professional life.

He was born in Stratford-on-Avon, a rural town in Warwickshire, England. The exact date of his birth is unknown, but he was baptized in Holy Trinity Church on April 26, 1564, and was probably born on April 23. His father, John Shakespeare, was a leather tanner, glover, alderman, and bailiff in the town. His mother, Mary, was the daughter of Robert Arden, a well-to-do gentleman farmer.

It is assumed that young William attended the Stratford Grammar School, one of the best in rural England, where he received a sound classical training. When he was 13, his father's fortunes took a turn for the worse, and it is likely that Shakespeare was apprenticed to some local trade as a butcher, killing calves. He may even have taught school for a time before he married Anne Hathaway, a woman eight years older than he, in 1582. Shakespeare was 18 years old at the time. Their oldest child, Susanna, was born and baptized six months later in May 1583. One year and nine months later, twins, Hamnet and Judith, were christened in the same church. They were named for Shakespeare's friends, Hamnet and Judith Sadler.

Little more is known about these early years, but in 1587 or 1588, he left Stratford and arrived in London to become an actor and a writer. By 1592, at the age of 28, he began to emerge as a playwright. He evoked criticism in a book published by playwright Robert Greene, who referred to Shakespeare as an "upstart crow" who is "in his own conceit the only Shake-scene in the country."

Shakespeare's first published work, the long poem *Venus and Adonis,* appeared in 1593. Its success was followed by another poem, *The Rape of Lucrece,* in 1594. These narrative poems were written in the years when the London theaters were closed because of the plague, a highly contagious disease that had devastated most of Europe.

In 1594, when the theaters reopened, records indicate that Shakespeare had become a leading member of the Lord Chamberlain's Men, a company of actors for which he wrote for the rest of his 20-year career.

It was in the 1590s that Shakespeare wrote his plays on English history, several comedies, and the tragedies *Titus Andronicus* and *Romeo and Juliet.* In 1599, the year he wrote *Julius Caesar,* Shakespeare's company built a theater across the Thames River from London—the Globe. Between 1600 and 1606, Shakespeare completed his major tragedies, *Hamlet, Othello, King Lear,* and *Macbeth.* His plays were performed at court for Queen Elizabeth I, and after her death in 1603, for King James I.

He wrote very little after 1612, the year that he completed *King Henry VIII.* It was during a performance of this play in 1613 that the Globe caught fire and burned to the ground. Sometime between 1610 and 1613, Shakespeare returned to Stratford, where he owned a large house and property, to spend his remaining years with his wife, two daughters and their husbands. Shakespeare's son, Hamnet, had died in 1596.

In March of 1616, Shakespeare revised his will, leaving his daughter Susanna the bulk of his estate, and his wife "the second best bed and the furniture." A month after his will was signed, on April 23, 1616, Shakespeare died—ironically, on his birthday, like Cassius in *Julius Caesar.* He was buried in the floor near the altar of Holy Trinity Church on April 25.

The wry inscription on his tombstone reads:

> Good Friend, for Jesus' sake, forbear
> To dig the dust enclosed here;
> Blest be the man that spares these stones
> And curst be he that moves my bones.

Historical Background

In 1599, when *Julius Caesar* was first performed, Queen Elizabeth I, the Tudor Queen, was in the final years of her 45-year reign (1558–1603). It was a period of history called the "Age of Discovery," a time of scientific growth, a rebirth of the arts, and exploration of the recently discovered continents of North and South America. Historical plays were popular during Shakespeare's lifetime and people were eager to learn about worlds other than their own. A play like *Julius Caesar* taught them about Roman history, and at the same time, provided them with a mirror of their own society—a peacetime monarchy after a hundred years of warfare and before the Civil War that began in 1642.

Elizabeth's reign was one of the most secure known by the English in hundreds of years. But her throne came under attack from Roman Catholic plots to replace the Protestant monarch with a Catholic. While Shakespeare was writing *Julius Caesar,* Elizabeth's own favorite, the Earl of Essex rebelled in 1601, intending to replace the Queen's Secretary of State, Sir Robert Cecil, with a group of young aristocrats. His plan failed. But even more damaging attacks on the idea of monarchy came from loyal Puritans. Radicals like Peter Wentworth and John Field wanted democracy and called for "liberty, freedom and enfranchisement," words echoed in Shakespeare's play.

Like Julius Caesar, Queen Elizabeth had no heirs to follow her on the throne. In 1599, when she was ill, people feared that civil war and religious struggle would be the only way the question of her succession could be answered.

Although Shakespeare was writing about Rome, he was also posing questions about his own times. Who is fit to have authority? Who is fit to take this authority away? Is authority justified by legal or divine right? Can rebellion against authority ever be justified? All of these concerns can be found in *Julius Caesar.*

Performance of the Play

In September of 1599, a Swiss doctor visiting London wrote in his journal that he crossed the Thames and "there in the thatched roof witnessed an excellent performance of the tragedy of the first emperor Julius." This entry is one of the few surviving pieces of information about the production in the original Globe Theater.

We know that a performance of *Julius Caesar* included realistic sound effects for thunder and battle scenes. The actor playing Caesar probably had a pig's bladder filled with blood under his costume, and when he was stabbed, he and the conspirators were covered with blood. About 15 men played all the parts in the play, memorizing several parts each. The two female roles were played by boy apprentices. There were no woman actors in the theater at this time.

Today critics are divided over *Julius Caesar*. Some consider it flawed because it is the only Shakespearean tragedy where the title character is killed halfway through the play. Also, the focus of the action is never clear. Who is the hero of the play? Is it Caesar or Brutus? What is the message Shakespeare intends? Certainly, they agree, the play is not as powerful as *Hamlet* or *King Lear*.

In reading the play today, we tend to judge it by our modern standards and concepts of democracy and freedom. When you read the play, try to see it through the eyes of one who lived in England at the beginning of the 17th Century. It was a time of change and discovery, yet it was a time of divine right, monarchy, order and obligation. Without these things the world would be in chaos. What destroys the harmony in Caesar's Rome—Caesar's ambition for power? Cassius' jealousy? Brutus' naivete? Or the fickleness of its citizens?

Master List of Characters

Julius Caesar—*Dictator of Rome*

Marcus Antonius (Mark Antony)—*Friend of Caesar and one of the leaders of Rome after Caesar's death*

Marcus Brutus—*Friend of Caesar who kills him "for the good of Rome"*

Cassius—*Leader of the conspiracy against Caesar and brother-in-law of Brutus*

Casca—*The first conspirator to stab Caesar*

Trebonius—*Member of the conspiracy against Caesar*

Caius Ligarius—*Final member of the conspiracy, a sick man who joins them when Brutus asks him to help make Rome well*

Decius Brutus—*Conspirator who uses flattery to get Caesar to the Senate House*

Metellus Cimber—*Conspirator and brother of Publius Cimber who was banished from Rome*

Cinna—*Conspirator who urges Cassius to bring Brutus into the conspiracy to gain favorable public opinion*

Flavius and Marullus—*Tribunes who guard the rights of Roman citizens*

Octavius Caesar—*Nephew of Julius Caesar and first Roman Emperor*

Lepidus—*Ally of Antony and Octavius and one of the three rulers of Rome after Caesar's assassination*

Cicero—*Roman senator and orator later killed by Antony, Octavius, and Lepidus*

Publius—*Elderly senator and witness to Caesar's death*

Popilius Lena—*Senator who was opposed to Caesar*

Calphurnia—*Wife of Caesar who tried to keep her husband home on the day of his assassination*

Portia—*Wife of Brutus, daughter of Cato and sister of Young Cato*

Lucilius—*Officer in Brutus' army who is captured by Antony*

Titinius—*Officer in Cassius' army who commits suicide after Cassius' death*

Messala—*Officer in Brutus' army who gives Brutus information from Rome, including news of Portia's suicide*

Young Cato—*Brother-in-law of Brutus who dies in battle*

Varro and Claudius—*Soldiers under Brutus' command who wait in his tent in Sardis before the battle at Philippi*

Volumnius, Clitus, and Dardanus—*Soldiers under Brutus' command who refuse to help him commit suicide after the battle of Philippi*

Strato—*Loyal friend of Brutus who assists him in his suicide*

Lucius—*Servant of Brutus*

Pindarus—*Servant of Cassius who helps his master commit suicide*

Artemidorus—*Friend of Caesar who writes a letter warning him of the plot*

Soothsayer—*Seer into the future who tries to warn Caesar about the plot to kill him*

Cinna the Poet—*Poet on his way to Caesar's funeral who is killed by an angry mob out for revenge*

Another Poet—*Jester who enters Brutus' tent while Brutus and Cassius are arguing*

Labeo and Flavius—*Soldiers in Brutus' army*

Summary of the Play

The play begins in Rome in 44 B.C. on the Feast of Lupercal, in honor of the god Pan. Caesar has become the most powerful man in the Roman Republic and is eager to become king. Caesar, however, has many enemies who are planning his assassination. When Caesar and his entourage appear, a soothsayer warns him to "Beware the ides of March," (March 15), but Caesar is unconcerned.

Cassius tries to convince Brutus that Caesar is too ambitious and must be assassinated for the welfare of Rome. Cassius is determined to win Brutus to his cause by forging letters from citizens and leaving them where Brutus will find them. The letters attack Caesar's ambition and convince Brutus that killing Caesar is for the good of Rome.

For a month, Brutus struggles with the problem and on the morning of the ides of March, he agrees to join the others. The conspirators escort Caesar to the Senate and stab him to death.

Brutus addresses the agitated crowd and tells them why Caesar had to be killed. Then Mark Antony delivers his funeral oration and stirs the crowd to mutiny against Brutus, Cassius, and the others. The mob runs through the streets looking to avenge Caesar's death. A civil war breaks out.

Brutus and Cassius escape to Greece where they raise an army and prepare to fight Octavius and Antony in a decisive battle.

When Cassius believes he has lost the war, he convinces his servant, Pindarus, to stab him. After Brutus is defeated in a second battle, he commits suicide by running on his own sword rather than being taken prisoner back to Rome.

The play ends with the restoration of order, as Octavius and Antony become the two most powerful men in Rome.

Estimated Reading Time

The play should take the reader about five hours to complete. Since it is a five-act play, you should allocate about an hour for each act, although the time may vary depending on the number of scenes in each act. The final two acts of the play read more quickly and they may be covered in less than an hour.

SECTION TWO

Act I

Act I, Scene I (pages 1–3)

New Characters:

Flavius and Marullus: *tribunes opposed to Caesar's growing power*

Roman Citizens: *among them a cobbler and carpenter, supporters of Caesar*

Summary

The setting is February 15, 44 B.C., the Feast of Lupercal, on a street in Rome. After the death of Pompey, Caesar has returned to Rome as the most powerful man in the Republic. The play begins on a Roman street with a confrontation between Flavius and Marullus (Roman tribunes) and a crowd of citizens out to celebrate Caesar's arrival for the games. The tribunes are concerned about Caesar's growing power and popular support and how it may destroy the Roman Republic. They scold the citizens and remind them of the love and support Rome once gave Pompey, who was killed in the civil war with Caesar. Flavius and Marullus drive the crowd from the streets. They decide to pull down any banners and decorations honoring Caesar, and scatter the crowds wherever they find them in an attempt to weaken popular support for Caesar.

Analysis

The opening scene is expository. It establishes the time and place and gives the audience an indication of what happened before the play began. It shows the political climate in Rome and the conflict surrounding Caesar. Rome, once ruled by three men (a *triumvirate*) is now in the hands of only one, Caesar, whose ambitions include becoming king. The citizens, once loyal to Pompey, one of the triumvirate, now form the base of Caesar's power. Others, represented by Flavius and Marullus, are opposed to Caesar and the threat he represents to the Roman Republic.

Flavius and Marullus drive the crowd from the streets. This shows how easily the crowd can be manipulated and controlled. Flavius and Marullus are concerned about the welfare of the Roman state and the negative impact that Caesar's lust for power will have on its citizens. Yet the crowd seems unconcerned about politics. They are only interested in having a holiday from work, and it does not seem to matter if the celebration is for Pompey or for Caesar.

This fickleness of the commoners will surface several times throughout the play. Ultimately the commoners are used as a force to affect the politics of Rome. This will become a significant factor later in the play.

Also significant are the issues of *interpretation* and *subjectivity*. Throughout the play a character's judgment is affected by another character's interpretation of events. In this scene Flavius and Marullus are able to influence the actions of the crowd by their accounts of Pompey and how good he was for Rome. This may or may not have been true, but their perception prevails in the scene. Look for other indications of this subjective interpretation of events as Brutus considers if he should kill Caesar, the interpretation of the meaning of omens in the play, and even Pindarus' report to Cassius of the capture of Titinius in Act V.

Note Shakespeare's use of the *pun*, a play on words, in the opening lines of this scene. "I am / but , as you would say, a cobbler." (p. 1) The word cobbler meant bungler as well as shoemaker. Later the character says, "all that I live by is with the / awl." Since Shakespeare's audience was often noisy and rowdy, he opens the scene with humorous wordplay to focus his audience's attention, make them laugh, and get them to listen. Once that has been done, he returns to the essential information in the scene—the developing conflict surrounding Caesar's growing ambition.

Study Questions

1. How does Shakespeare use humor in the opening scene?

2. A pun is a play on words, two words that sound alike but have different meanings. Find two examples of puns in the opening lines of the scene.

3. How does Shakespeare show the political conflict in Rome?

4. What is the reason the cobbler tells Flavius and Marullus he is leading the people through the street?

5. What is the real reason the people are out in the street?

6. What about Pompey is revealed in this scene?

7. What information is given about Caesar?

8. How does the scene show the fickleness of the crowd?

9. Shakespeare often uses comparisons (metaphor and simile) and figurative language. What is the comparison Flavius makes in the final lines of the scene?

10. What are the intentions of Flavius and Marullus as the scene ends?

Answers

1. His characters pun, or play with word meanings. They use words that sound alike but have different meanings.

2. The word "cobbler" has two meanings, shoemaker and bungler. A "mender of bad soles" is a reference to shoemaker. This is a play on the word "souls."

    An awl is a leather punch. It is used with the word "all." Recover means to repair, as in repair shoes. Recover also means to get better as from an illness.

3. He does this by opening the play with a confrontation between the tribunes and the citizens, two opposing forces in Rome.

4. The cobbler wants them to wear out their shoes so he will get more work.

5. They are out to see Caesar and rejoice in his triumph.

6. Pompey was once loved and respected by the people of Rome.

7. Caesar was responsible for Pompey's death.

8. Flavius and Marullus are able to change the mind of the crowd with their words and convince them to disperse.

9. He compares Caesar to a bird. Driving the crowd from the street will be like plucking feathers from a bird's wing so it can not fly high.

10. They plan to go through the streets and pull down any banners that honor Caesar.

Suggested Essay Topics

1. Read through Caesar's *Commentaries*, an account of his battles in Europe and write a brief history of Caesar's rise to power.

2. Research the first triumvirate—Caesar, Crassus and Pompey. What happened to it? What were the causes and the results of the Roman Civil War?

3. The tribunes Flavius and Marullus are concerned about Caesar's rise to power. Research the role of the tribunes in Roman society and discuss their duties and responsibilities.

Act I, Scene II (pages 3–12)

New Characters:

Caesar: *the most powerful man in the Roman Republic after the death of Pompey*

Calphurnia: *Caesar's wife*

Brutus: *friend of Caesar, concerned about the welfare of Rome*

Cassius: *brother-in-law of Brutus and leader of the conspiracy against Caesar*

Casca: *a conspirator against Caesar*

Antony: *a close friend of Caesar*

Soothsayer: *one who sees the future and tries to warn Caesar*

Summary

The setting for this scene is another Roman street on the Feast of Lupercal. Caesar enters at the head of a procession (triumph) with a flourish of trumpets, accompanied by his wife, friends, and some of the conspirators who will later stab him to death. They are on their way to the Coliseum for the traditional footrace to celebrate the Feast of Lupercal, a fertility festival in honor of the god Pan. Caesar stops the procession and calls for Calphurnia. He then orders Antony, who is dressed to run, to touch Calphurnia during the race. The Romans believed that a barren (sterile) woman touched by the winner of the race on the Feast of Lupercal would "Shake off their sterile curse." As they are about to move off, a soothsayer calls to Caesar from the crowd. He warns Caesar, "Beware the ides of March." (March 15) (p. 4) But Caesar dismisses the man as "a dreamer" and the procession continues to the Coliseum.

Cassius and Brutus remain behind. Cassius voices his concern about Brutus' seeming coolness toward him. Brutus assures Cassius that they are still friends, explaining to Cassius that he is simply distracted. During their conversation they hear three shouts from the Coliseum, and Brutus admits he is afraid the people have chosen Caesar to be king.

Cassius then begins his campaign to undermine Caesar and his growing power. He tells Brutus that the Romans have allowed

Caesar to grow too powerful and tries to show Brutus why Caesar is unfit to rule Rome. Cassius says he once saved Caesar from drowning during a swimming race, and another time he saw Caesar with a fever, crying "As a sick girl." (p. 7) Cassius appeals to Brutus to do something before Caesar destroys the Roman Republic. Brutus says he will not live under the control of a king, and he is even ready to die for the good of Rome.

After the games end, Caesar and his entourage return. When he sees Cassius and Brutus together he recognizes the potential threat that Cassius represents. He tells Antony, "Yond Cassius has a lean and hungry look; / He thinks too much: such men are dangerous." (p. 9) He says that Cassius is never at "heart's ease" when he is in the company of someone who is better than he (Caesar). But Caesar quickly dismisses the threat posed by Cassius "for always I am Caesar."

Casca, cynical and sarcastic, describes to Brutus and Cassius what happened at the Coliseum. The crowd cheered when Antony presented Caesar with a crown three times, which Caesar refused each time. According to Casca's account, the people cheered so much that their bad breath knocked Caesar down and he passed out. Brutus, however, says that Caesar has epilepsy.

Before he fell, Casca says, Caesar told the crowd that they could cut his throat if he displeased them, and Casca says he would have done it if he had a knife. When he recovered from his seizure, Caesar apologized for his words and actions, winning the forgiveness and sympathies of the crowd. Casca also tells Cassius and Brutus that Flavius and Marullus "for pulling scarfs off Caesar's images, are put to silence." (p. 11) This might mean they were put out of office, imprisoned, or even put to death.

Cassius recognizes Casca as another potential ally against Caesar and invites him to supper. He tells Brutus to consider all the things they have discussed. When Cassius is alone he says in a *soliloquy* (a speech made by a character who is alone on the stage) that he will write letters in different handwriting and leave them where Brutus will find them. He hopes the letters will convince Brutus that public opinion is opposed to Caesar, and move Brutus to take action.

Analysis

This scene shows Caesar's power and the attitudes of those surrounding him. This is done through Caesar's words in the opening lines, the reactions of others to him, and what others say about him. Caesar is vain, insensitive, and conceited. He humiliates his wife by publicly calling attention to her sterility. Yet Antony jumps when Caesar gives him an order. Antony responds, "When Caesar says 'do this,' it is perform'd." (p. 4) Caesar seems to be afraid of nothing. He dismisses the soothsayer as a "dreamer." This inflated opinion of himself will resurface later in the scene and several other times in the play.

The scene reveals that Brutus is troubled by Caesar's rise to power. This concern has preoccupied him to the point that he has neglected his friends. Brutus is at war with himself.

If there is a villain in the play, it is Cassius. He is jealous of Caesar and aware that Brutus can be manipulated by what he perceives to be for the good of Rome. Cassius probes Brutus by asking if he is aware of what is happening in Rome. When Brutus reacts to the shouts from the crowd, Cassius steps up his attack on Caesar. His story about saving Caesar's life may or may not be true. Angrily he points out that Caesar has become a god and that he must bow to him.

The issue of subjective interpretation is significant in this scene. Although Brutus is already considering the potential threat Caesar poses to Rome, it is Cassius' perception of Caesar that adds to Brutus' concern. Is Caesar really as great a threat as Cassius says?

When Caesar reappears, his astute political judgment is revealed when he immediately recognizes the threat that Cassius poses. He assesses Cassius as a loner who doesn't sleep, who reads, and who is generally not content with his life. Caesar knows instinctively that if any man is to be feared, it is Cassius. Yet Caesar is afraid of nothing. This pride, coupled with ambition, blinds him and makes him vulnerable. Caesar wishes to be a god, but, ironically, he suffers from certain physical afflictions. He is deaf in his left ear, and he is an epileptic.

The cynical and sarcastic Casca gives a humorous and biased account of the events that occurred at the Coliseum, revealing his own feelings toward Caesar. Caesar played to the crowd by three times refusing Antony's offer of a coronet, a small crown. Caesar may have done this because the crown offered by Antony was only symbolic, and had no power connected with it. By refusing the crown, Caesar would show the crowd that he wasn't really ambitious. According to Casca, when the crowd cheered, their bad breath knocked Caesar down. In actuality Caesar suffered an epileptic seizure. Brutus calls it "the falling-sickness." Cassius makes a pun, indicating that Rome has "the falling-sickness," (p. 10) falling down in worship before Caesar.

Casca's attitude, his account of the events and his reference to cutting Caesar's throat, indicate to that he is another candidate for the growing plot against Caesar. Cassius invites Casca to supper to recruit him into the conspiracy. Casca's news that Flavius and Marullus were silenced is another indication of Caesar's possible abuse of power.

Cassius' soliloquy is an important aspect of this scene. A soliloquy, a speech made by a character who is alone on the stage, reveals the character's true nature, thoughts, and feelings. In his soliloquy, after Casca and Brutus exit, Cassius indicates how he plans to trick Brutus into the plot against Caesar. He will forge letters indicating that Rome wants Caesar killed, and leave them where Brutus will find them. Cassius is shrewd, calculating, and ready to take advantage of Brutus for his own political and personal reasons. He knows that Brutus is well-respected in Rome, and his joining the conspiracy will give it respectability.

Study Questions

1. How is Caesar's power indicated in the scene?
2. What was the soothsayer's warning?
3. What reason does Brutus give Cassius for his coolness towards him?
4. What two stories does Brutus tell about Caesar?
5. What does Cassius compare Caesar to in lines 142–45?
6. What reasons does Caesar give Antony that Cassius is dangerous?
7. Why does Casca say Caesar fell?

8. What does Brutus mean when he says Caesar has the "falling sickness"?

9. What does Cassius mean when he says, "But you, and I, / And honest Casca, we have the falling-sickness"? (p. 10)

10. How does Cassius plan to trick Brutus into joining the plot against Caesar?

Answers

1. When he tells Antony to touch Calphurnia in the race, Antony says, "When Caesar says 'do this,' it is perform'd."

2. The Soothsayer warns, "Beware of the ides of March."

3. Brutus says that he has some private matters on his mind that are troubling him.

4. Caesar challenged Cassius to a swimming race, and Cassius had to save his life. He also saw Caesar with the fever in Spain, crying like "a sick girl."

5. He compares Caesar to a giant statue, under whose legs Romans must walk.

6. He is too thin. He is lean and hungry for power. He doesn't sleep. He reads. He is an observer. He doesn't smile or go to plays or listen to music. He thinks too much.

7. Casca says that the bad breath of the crowd knocked Caesar down.

8. Caesar suffers from epilepsy.

9. Cassius means that Romans are falling down before Caesar's power.

10. Cassius plans to forge letters and leave them where Brutus will find them. The letters will convince Brutus that public sentiment is against Caesar.

Suggested Essay Topics

1. Read Plutarch's *The Life of Caesar* and compare his account of the historical events with the events as they are depicted in Shakespeare's play.

2. History has been touched by political assassinations from Abraham Lincoln to Martin Luther King, Jr. Very often the profile of the assassin is that of a loner, a misfit, who has no friends and does not conform to the norms of society. Choose one political assassination and research the life and personality of the person responsible. Compare him to the picture Shakespeare presents of Cassius in the play.

Act I, Scene III (pages 12–17)

New Characters:

Cicero: *a Roman senator and orator*

Cinna: *a conspirator against Caesar*

Summary

It is the night before the ides of March, and a terrible storm is raging. A frightened Casca, with his sword drawn, meets Cicero on a Roman street. Casca describes to Cicero all the unusual things he has witnessed: heaven "dropping fire," (p. 13) a man with his hand ablaze but not burning, a lion in the Capitol, an owl hooting in the marketplace at noon, and men on fire walking through the streets. Casca interprets all these signs to mean either the gods are engaged in civil war, or they are determined to destroy Rome. They mention Caesar's plans to be at the Capitol in the morning, and Cicero exits as Cassius enters.

Cassius is unconcerned about the storm and tells Casca that he has been daring the lightning to strike him. When Casca says all these terrible things are signs from the gods, Cassius interprets them as warnings against Caesar. Casca reveals that the senators plan to make Caesar king, and give him a crown that he may wear "every place save here in Italy." (p. 15) Cassius says he would rather kill himself than see Caesar made king. He tells Casca of a plot to kill Caesar, and convinces him to join the conspiracy.

Cinna, another conspirator, enters and reports to Cassius that the others are waiting for him at Pompey's Porch, the covered entrance to the theater built by Pompey. Cassius gives Cinna some letters and instructs him to leave them where Brutus will find them. When Cinna leaves, Cassius tells Casca that Brutus is almost convinced to join them, and that one final push "yields him ours." Casca rightly states that Brutus is well-respected in Rome, and his joining the conspiracy will give it respectability. Act I ends with them heading for Brutus' house to "awake him and be sure of him." (p.17)

Analysis

A month has passed, and there is a storm raging, symbolizing the political storm unfolding in Rome. Caesar, the head of state, is on the brink of assassination, and the natural order in Roman society is being threatened. Casca, like many Romans, is superstitious. He interprets these unusual events as evil omens. The gods, he thinks, are bent on destroying Rome.

Cassius sees Caesar's unbridled power as a greater evil and the surest way to destroying the Roman Republic. In his meeting with Casca, he reveals himself to be unafraid and undisturbed by events. Cassius is confident, openly daring the lightning to strike him. His mood is almost joyful as he and the other conspirators plan to rid Rome of a tyrant. Cassius calls the evening "A very pleasing night to honest men," (p. 14) indicating that he regards his plans to kill Caesar as just and necessary. Cassius uses a similar approach to discover Casca's feelings toward Caesar and recruit him into his plot as he did with Brutus. He tells Casca that Romans have grown weak and "womanish" as Caesar has grown strong. His words are convincing and Casca, with a handshake, joins Cassius and the others against Caesar.

When Cinna arrives, Cassius identifies the other conspirators by name. Decius Brutus (not to be confused with Marcus Brutus), Trebonius, and Metellus Cimber are among them. The letters Cassius gives to Cinna are those he mentioned in his soliloquy. In the course of the month that has passed, many letters have been posted where Brutus would find them. They have had the desired effect of convincing Brutus of a public sentiment against Caesar. Cassius says of Brutus, "Three parts of him / Is ours already, and the man entire / Upon the next encounter yields him ours." (p. 17) The importance of having Brutus with them is also understood by Casca who says, "O, he sits high in all the people's hearts; / And that which would appear offence in us / His countenance, like richest alchemy, / Will change to virtue and to worthiness." (p. 17)

   In this scene Cassius introduces the idea of suicide. He says he will kill himself before he will see Caesar made king. Elizabethan England was generally opposed to the concept of suicide, because it went against the Christian teaching that only God could take a person's life. However, the notion of suicide among Romans, as in the Japanese samurai tradition, was acceptable. Many Romans considered suicide preferable to dishonor and defeat. This will become a significant factor in Act V.

Study Questions

1. Why does Casca have his sword drawn?
2. What two "supernatural" events does Casca describe to Cicero?
3. What unusual "natural" event does he tell about?
4. Why does Casca think these unusual things are happening?
5. What information about Caesar is revealed in their conversation?
6. How is Cassius' conduct in the storm different from Casca's?
7. How does Cassius interpret all that is happening in Rome?
8. What news does Cinna bring to Cassius?
9. Why does Casca think it is important for Brutus to join with them in the plot against Caesar?
10. How does Cassius plan to put extra pressure on Brutus at the end of Act I?

Answers

1. He passed a lion walking in the streets of the Capitol.
2. A slave with his hands on fire was not burned. Men on fire were walking through the streets.

3. An owl, the bird of night, sat hooting in the marketplace at midday.

4. The gods are either at war or are trying to destroy the world.

5. He is going to the Capitol in the morning on the ides of March.

6. He is unafraid because he is an honest man. He even dares the lightning to strike him.

7. He says the gods are warning Romans against Caesar.

8. The other conspirators are assembled at Pompey's Porch and they are awaiting Cassius.

9. Public opinion of Brutus is favorable, and he will make the killing of Caesar seem like a noble act.

10. He and Casca and the others plan to go to his house and press him to join them.

Suggested Essay Topics

1. Superstition is an important part of the play and a significant factor in Roman life. Examine the superstition and the supernatural events described in this scene. Research Roman mythology and Roman superstitions. What did the Romans believe and what were they afraid of?

2. Compare the character of Casca as he is depicted in Scenes I and II. How has he changed? What does the audience learn from him and why is he an important character in the play?

SECTION THREE

Act II

Act II, Scene I (pages 18–28)

New Characters:

Lucius: *Brutus' servant*

Decius: *conspirator who plans to flatter Caesar and bring him to the Senate House*

Metellus Cimber and Trebonius: *conspirators against Caesar*

Portia: *wife of Brutus*

Caius Ligarius: *ill friend of Brutus; the last to join the conspiracy*

Summary

The setting for the scene is before three o'clock in the morning of the ides of March, and Brutus is alone in his garden. He is unable to sleep. His mind is still disturbed as he wrestles with what to do about Caesar. In a soliloquy, Brutus considers the possibilities. He has no personal feelings against Caesar, yet he must consider the good of Rome. Caesar has not yet acted irresponsibly, but once he is crowned and has power, he could change and do harm to Rome. Brutus compares Caesar to a poisonous snake. Because Caesar may be corrupted by power, Brutus decides he must be prevented from gaining power. He says, "And therefore think him as a serpent's egg / Which hatch'd would as his kind grow mischievous, / And kill him in the shell." (p. 19) Lucius, Brutus' servant, brings him some letters he has found. They all urge Brutus to act against Caesar.

Cassius, Casca, Cinna, Decius, Metellus Cimber, and Trebonius arrive to put more pressure on Brutus. Brutus announces his intention to join them, taking charge. First he convinces the others that they don't need Cicero in the conspiracy, and then he convinces them that Antony should not be killed with Caesar. Brutus tells Metellus to send Caius Ligarius, who has a grudge against Caesar, to see him so that Brutus may bring him into the plot. Decius says that he will use flattery to get Caesar out of his house if he decides to remain home. They leave with plans to arrive at Caesar's house at eight o'clock to escort him to the Capitol.

After they are gone, Portia, Brutus' wife, appears and begs him to confide in her what is going on. She convinces him that although she is a woman, she is strong and capable of keeping his secrets. But just as Brutus is about to tell Portia everything, an ill Ligarius arrives. Because he has such regard for Brutus, Ligarius agrees to "discard [his] sickness" (p. 28) and follow Brutus. Brutus leads Ligarius towards Caesar's house, revealing the details of their plans as they go.

Analysis

For a month Brutus has been wrestling with his thoughts, unable to eat or sleep. Lucius, in contrast, has no difficulty falling asleep. In Shakespeare's world, sleep is reserved only for the innocent, those with untroubled minds.

While pacing in his garden Brutus decides that Caesar must be killed, not for what Caesar *is*, but for what he *may* become. His decision to kill Caesar has nothing to do with a desire for personal gain or power. Brutus is driven purely by concern for the good of Rome. He regards Caesar, his friend, as a potential threat to the well-being of the Republic. He compares Caesar to a poisonous snake that is dangerous only after it is hatched. To prevent danger, it must be killed in the shell. So Caesar must be killed before he abuses his power. The letters presented by Lucius, left by Cinna at the direction of Cassius, only reaffirm what Brutus has already decided.

When the other conspirators arrive, Brutus joins them with a handshake and commits himself to their plan to kill Caesar. Immediately he becomes their new leader, replacing Cassius. Ironically, the man who does not want power takes over, making decisions for these men throughout the rest of the play. He convinces them that they need not swear an oath to their cause, because what they are about to do is noble and important enough to bind them together.

When Metellus and the others want Cicero in the conspiracy to "purchase us a good opinion, / And buy men's voices to commend our deeds," (p. 23) Brutus persuades them that Cicero is unnecessary, "For he will never follow any thing / That other men begin."

When the question of killing Antony is brought up by the practical Cassius, Brutus again prevails. He says that they are "sacrificers, but not butchers," and convinces them that if they kill Antony, their "course will seem too bloody." It would be like cutting off Caesar's head and afterwards hacking off his arms and legs.

Cassius' desire to kill Antony, however, is based on sound political considerations. Antony, a friend of Caesar, might later cause trouble for the conspirators. Cassius rightly concludes that Antony should be killed with Caesar. The idealistic Brutus is moved by what he perceives to be right, and to him killing Antony would be wrong. His speech on pages 23–24 convinces them to let Antony live. This error, and other errors in judgment made by Brutus in Act III, will later prove disastrous.

The matter of Caesar's superstition arises when Cassius questions whether Caesar will even leave his house while so many strange phenomena are occurring. Decius says he will take advantage of Caesar's vulnerability to flattery to persuade Caesar to come to the Capitol.

As the conspirators leave, determined to meet at Caesar's house by eight o'clock, Portia enters. She begs Brutus to share his problems with her as his true wife. She kneels, telling him that even though she is a woman, she is strong enough to keep his secrets. To prove this she even gives herself a voluntary wound in the thigh without crying out. Brutus is so moved by Portia's display that he says he is not worthy of such a wife. The only thing that prevents him from telling her everything is the arrival of Caius Ligarius. In a very brief exchange with Ligarius, the esteem in which Brutus is held by his peers is revealed. The ill Ligarius ignores his own sickness because Brutus needs him for some undisclosed enterprise. It is a testimonial to the high opinion Ligarius and Rome have of Brutus.

Note Shakespeare's use of *anachronisms* (an object or event from the wrong time period) in this scene. Shakespeare was not concerned about the historical accuracy of certain details, and he mixed events from his era with those from Roman times. Sometimes these anachronisms were convenient methods to move the play along. How would the conspirators account for the time if the clock didn't strike three? (Clocks did not exist in Caesar's time.) Lucius tells Brutus that he does not recognize the men at the gate because they are wearing hats and cloaks. Neither hats nor cloaks were part of the Roman dress, but were in the 1600s. In addition, kerchiefs were worn by sick men and women in Shakespeare's England. Look for other anachronisms in the course of the play.

Study Questions

1. What reason does Brutus give in his soliloquy for killing Caesar?
2. What do the letters addressed to Brutus say?
3. Why can't Lucius identify the men with Cassius?
4. Why does Brutus oppose the idea of swearing an oath?
5. Why does Brutus object to Cicero joining the conspiracy?
6. Why does Brutus oppose killing Mark Antony?
7. How does Decius plan to get Caesar to the Capitol?
8. What advice does Brutus give the conspirators as they leave his house?
9. Why does Portia think she is strong enough to share in Brutus' plans?
10. How does Caius Ligarius prove his high regard for Brutus?

Answers

1. Brutus justifies killing Caesar for the good of Rome, fearing that he may abuse his power.
2. The letters urge him to "speak, strike and redress," to act against Caesar.

3. The men have their hats pulled down and their cloaks pulled up so their faces are hidden.

4. Brutus feels their cause is good enough to bind them together, and if it is not, they might as well go home and wait for death to take them.

5. He says Cicero will never follow what someone else began.

6. Their cause would seem too bloody, and they would be considered murderers. He thinks Antony is not dangerous.

7. He says he will use flattery.

8. He tells them to look fresh and hide their plans by smiling so their appearances won't give them away.

9. Portia is the daughter of Cato and the wife of Brutus, and she gave herself a voluntary wound in the thigh without crying out.

10. Ligarius agrees to do whatever Brutus needs him to do without knowing what it may be, even though he is sick.

Suggested Essay Topics

1. Read Plutarch's *Life of Brutus* and compare the historical account of Brutus to the character in Shakespeare's play.

2. A "tragic flaw" is a weakness of personality in a character that makes the character vulnerable, and leads to his destruction. What were Caesar's and Brutus' "tragic flaws" and how do these flaws make them vulnerable?

Act II, Scene II (pages 28–32)

Summary

It is almost eight o'clock in the morning on the ides of March at Caesar's house. Caesar is awakened by Calphurnia crying out in her sleep. Caesar orders his servant to have the priests sacrifice an animal and bring back word of the results. Calphurnia asks her husband to stay at home because she is afraid he will be murdered, but the proud and haughty Caesar refuses to take her warning.

Caesar's servant returns with word from the augurers (priests), who want Caesar to remain inside because, "They could not find a heart within the beast." (p. 29)

Caesar interprets this differently. He says, "The gods do this in shame of cowardice. / Caesar should be a beast without a heart / If he should stay at home today for fear." (pp. 29–30) It is only when Calphurnia kneels and begs him to stay home for her sake that Caesar agrees.

As planned, Decius arrives to escort Caesar to the Senate. Caesar tells him to take word to the senators that he intends to remain home. When Decius presses him for a reason, Caesar tells him of Calphurnia's dream, where she saw a statue of Caesar oozing blood in a hundred places, with many Romans bathing their hands in it. However, Decius interprets the dream in a favorable way. He says that Caesar is the lifeblood of Rome, and the men bathing in his blood are gaining strength from him. Decius also appeals to Caesar's pride. He tells him that the senators might think Caesar is afraid if he does not show up because Calphurnia had bad dreams. Decius' appeal changes Caesar's mind. He decides to ignore his wife's fears and go to the Senate. Brutus, Cassius, and the others arrive in time to put more pressure on Caesar. The scene ends with them leaving together for the Senate House.

Analysis

This scene parallels the preceding scene, where Portia influences Brutus, only to be interrupted by Ligarius. Here Calphurnia convinces Caesar to stay at home, only to have Decius interrupt, changing Caesar's mind.

Superstition and supernatural forces again play an important part in this scene. In an attempt to convince her husband to stay home, Calphurnia describes fantastic events she has witnessed or heard about, and interprets them as omens meant to warn Caesar. She tells of graves yielding up their dead, a lioness giving birth in the streets of the city, and blood dripping from the clouds onto the Capitol, events similar to those extraordinary occurrences mentioned earlier by Casca. Calphurnia pleads with Caesar to give into her fears. "Caesar, I never stood on ceremonies, / Yet now they fright me." (p. 29) But because of his pride, Caesar is unmoved. He says, "Cowards die many times before their deaths; / The valiant never taste of death but once." (p. 29) When his servant brings word that the augurers could not find a heart in the beast they sacrificed, Caesar interprets it to mean the gods would consider him a coward without a heart if he does not go to the Senate. It is only when Calphurnia kneels to him, as Portia did with Brutus, that he consents. For an instant a tender and human side of Caesar is revealed. But when Calphurnia tells Caesar to say he is sick, it is too much for his pride to lie to "greybeards." When he does agree to send Decius to the Senate with his decision, Caesar says, "Tell them that I will not come to-day. / Cannot, is false, and that I dare not, falser: / I will not come to-day." (p. 30) It must be made clear to the senators that Caesar is in control.

After hearing Calphurnia's dream, Decius interprets it in a favorable way. He says it is a good omen, that Caesar is the center of Rome and from him "great Rome shall suck / Reviving blood." (p. 31) He convinces Caesar to go by telling him that the Senate plans to give him a crown, and they may change their mind if Caesar does not come. There are those who will laugh at Caesar and think him a coward if he hides himself at home because Calphurnia had bad dreams. This is too much for Caesar to bear, and he changes his mind once again and agrees to go to the Senate. The man who says he hates flatterers is flattered and lured to his death.

Study Questions

1. Why is Caesar concerned when the scene begins?

2. What is Calphurnia's request of Caesar?

3. What is Caesar's response to Calphurnia's concern he might be killed?

4. What was the result of the sacrifice performed by the augurers?

5. What reasons does Caesar give Decius for staying home?

6. What was Calphurnia's dream?

7. How does Decius use flattery to get Caesar to change his mind?

8. How does Decius interpret Calphurnia's dream?

9.   What does Trebonius say when Caesar tells him to stay by?

10. What is the irony in Caesar's last lines in the scene?

Answers

1.   A storm is raging and Calphurnia had a dream that Caesar was murdered.

2.   She wants him to stay at home. Calphurnia is afraid for his safety because of the unusual events that are going on and because of her dream.

3.   Caesar's response is, "Cowards die many times before their deaths; / The valiant never taste of death but once."

4.   The augurers could not find a heart in the beast they sacrificed and they want Caesar to stay at home.

5.   Caesar tells Decius that he is staying home because Calphurnia wants him to.

6.   Calphurnia dreamed a statue of Caesar was spouting blood and Romans were washing their hands in it.

7.   Decius interprets Calphurnia's dream in a favorable way. He tells Caesar that people will think Caesar is a coward if he doesn't go to the Senate House. He says the senate may change their minds about giving Caesar a crown.

8.   Caesar is the lifeblood of Rome, and Romans, bathing in his blood, derive strength from him.

9.   He says, in an aside, that he will stay so close that Caesar's friends will wish Trebonius had been further away.

10. He regards the conspirators as friends, having no idea they plan to kill him within the hour.

Suggested Essay Topics

1.   Compare Caesar in Act I, Scene II to the Caesar that appears in this scene. How is he the same? How is he different? What does he fear and what are the forces that influence him?

2.   Wives play a key role in Act II, Scenes I and II. How do the wives of Brutus and Caesar try to influence their husbands? Are they successful?

Act II, Scenes III–IV (pages 32–34)

New Character:

Artemidorus: *teacher and friend of some of the conspirators; he has learned about the plot against Caesar*

Summary

The setting is a Roman street on the ides of March shortly before the planned assassination. Artemidorus, a teacher and friend of some of the conspirators, has learned about the plot to kill Caesar. He has written a letter naming each man and warning Caesar to be on his guard. He plans to wait for Caesar to pass and then present the letter as a suitor looking for a political favor.

At the same time, on another part of the street, an agitated Portia tells Lucius to run to the Capitol and report back to her everything his master, Brutus, says and does. The confused boy is unsure of what the distracted Portia wants him to do and he hesitates. When Portia sees the soothsayer passing by his way to the Capitol, she asks him if he knows about any harm intended toward Caesar. The soothsayer responds, "None that I know will be, much that I fear may chance." (Sc. IV, p. 34) He tells her that he plans to speak to Caesar when he passes.

In an aside, Portia wishes Brutus success in his enterprise and she sends Lucius off on his errand.

Analysis

How Artemidorus learned about the plot is not explained, but his information is correct and up-to-date. His list of conspirators includes Ligarius, who joined Brutus only recently. His letter cautions Caesar against overconfidence. "If thou beest not immortal, look about you: security gives way to conspiracy." (Sc. III, p. 32) It is precisely Caesar's sense of his own immortality, his attitude that he *is* a god, that makes him so vulnerable.

Portia's behavior in Scene IV indicates that she knows what is about to occur. Because Shakespeare does not say exactly how she knows, we must assume she has either been told by Brutus, or has figured it out for herself. The issue of her being a "weak" woman, brought up in the previous scene, is mentioned again. "O constancy, be strong upon my side! / Set a huge mountain 'tween my heart and tongue! / I have a man's mind, but a woman's might. / How hard it is for women to keep counsel!" (Sc. IV, p. 33) Portia is now so agitated she can hardly contain herself, and is about to burst. Her orders to Lucius are unclear and his response is almost humorous. "Madam, what should I do? / Run to the Capitol, and nothing else? / And so return to you, and nothing else?" (Sc. IV, p. 33). Her exchange with the soothsayer makes it clear she knows there is a plot to "harm" Caesar.

Since all of the roles in Shakespeare's plays were acted by males, Portia's comment about a man's mind and a woman's might is a joke that wouldn't have been missed by the audience in the Globe Theater.

Study Questions

1. How does Shakespeare add the element of suspense in these two short scenes?

2. What is Artemidorus' warning?

3. What does Artemidorus mean when he says, "Security gives way to conspiracy"? (Sc. III, p. 32)

4. How does he plan to give Caesar his letter?

5. Why doesn't Lucius carry out Portia's request?

6. What does Portia mean in her aside, "O constancy, be strong upon my side!/ Set a huge mountain 'tween my heart and tongue! / I have a man's mind, but a woman's might. / How hard it is for women to keep counsel!" (Sc. IV, p. 33)?

7. What does she tell Lucius to do?

8. What does the soothsayer tell Portia he plans to do?

9. What is Portia's wish for Brutus?

10. How does Portia try to cover up being overheard by Lucius?

Answers

1. He provides Caesar with two possibilities of saving his life: through Artemidorus' letter or the soothsayer.

2. Artemidorus warns Caesar to be on his guard if he is not immortal.

3. He means that overconfidence on Caesar's part opens the way to conspiracy and death.

4. He will wait on the street as a suitor looking for some political favor and present the letter to Caesar when he passes.

5. Portia does not make her intentions clear.

6. She is afraid she will not be able to keep Brutus' plans a secret because she is a "weak" woman.

7. Portia tells Lucius to bring back word as to how Brutus looks, what Caesar does, and which suitors present themselves to Caesar.

8. He will go down the street and speak to Caesar when he comes by and try to warn him about the possible danger.

9. She hopes the heavens will help him in his enterprise.

10. She tells him Brutus has a suit (a request) that Caesar will not grant him.

Suggested Essay Topics

1. Rome was a republic that depended on slavery similar to the United States until the 1860s. Research the history of slavery in Rome. Where did the slaves come from? What roles did they play in the Republic? What was a slave's life like? What rights and responsibilities did they have? What were the rights and responsibilities of Roman citizens?

2. Compare the characters of Calphurnia and Portia in terms of how they are portrayed by Shakespeare in this act. How are the two women similar? Compare the two scenes involving these two wives and their husbands. What purpose do the scenes serve?

SECTION FOUR

Act III

Act III, Scene I (pages 35–44)

New Characters:

Lepidus: *one of the three rulers of Rome after Caesar's death*

Publius: *elderly Roman senator who escorts Caesar to the Senate*

Popilius Lena: *senator who wishes success to Cassius*

Servant: *messenger from Octavius*

Summary

Caesar arrives at the Senate House on the ides of March. Artemidorus tries to give Caesar his warning letter, as Decius offers Caesar a petition. Artemidorus presses Caesar to read his letter first because it "touches Caesar nearer." (p. 35) Caesar responds, "What touches us ourself shall be last served." (p. 35) In other words, he ignores the letter because it is of a personal nature. Cassius is afraid that their plans are known when Popilius, a senator, says to him, "I wish your enterprise to-day may thrive." (p. 35)

Cassius tells Casca to act quickly. Trebonius, as prearranged, removes Antony from the scene. Under the pretext of begging repeal of a banishment decree imposed by Caesar on Publius Cimber, brother of Metellus, they surround Caesar and isolate him from the rest of the senators. As Caesar rejects each of their appeals, the conspirators tighten the circle around him. Casca is the first to strike, and, after each of the conspirators attack Caesar, Brutus is the last to stab him. Mortally wounded, Caesar says his last words, "*Et tu, Brutè*? Then fall, Caesar!" (p. 37) and dies.

Panic ensues as the senators run from the Senate House. Under the direction of Brutus, the conspirators bathe their hands and swords in Caesar's blood and prepare to go into the streets. But before they can tell the Romans what has happened, Antony's servant enters and begs for permission for his master to come and speak to all of them. Brutus agrees, but before Antony's arrival, Cassius again considers the possibility of killing Antony.

When Antony arrives he tells the conspirators that he is ready to die, if that is their plan. Brutus assures Antony that there is no harm intended toward him, or anyone else. Reassured by Brutus, Antony shakes their bloody hands and asks for permission to bring Caesar's body to the marketplace and to speak at Caesar's funeral. Again Brutus is quick to agree, and again Cassius objects. Brutus overrides the objection and tells Antony that he may speak, but only with certain restrictions. Antony may not blame the conspirators for killing Caesar, although he may say good things about Caesar. He must say he speaks by permission from the same pulpit after Brutus speaks.

After they leave, Antony declares his true feelings in a powerful soliloquy. He predicts a violent and bloody civil war, and he vows revenge for Caesar's death. A messenger arrives with news that young Octavius, Caesar's nephew, has arrived outside of Rome. Antony tells the messenger to wait until after his funeral speech, and then return to Octavius with news as to whether or not it is safe or not for him to enter Rome. Together they carry Caesar's body to the marketplace.

Analysis

Time is running out for Caesar, but there are still two possibilities that may save his life. The first is the soothsayer and the other is Artemidorus. Caesar dismisses the soothsayer when he sees him with his mocking, "The ides of March are come." (p. 35) Then, he ignores Artemidorus' letter because it is personal business. Ironically, this man who regards himself as a god, who identifies himself as the center of Rome, who uses the words "us ourself" when he refers to himself, cuts himself off from possible salvation by putting himself last.

Fearing detection because their security has been compromised, Cassius indicates he will kill himself rather than live under

Caesar. But it becomes clear that Popilius, a senator who wishes Cassius well, does not intend to warn Caesar, and the conspirators are free to carry out their plan. Trebonius is the only conspirator who doesn't stab Caesar. His purpose is to lead Antony off and prevent him from coming to Caesar's aid.

As he begins the day's proceedings, Caesar's ego is apparent. He says, "What is now amiss / That Caesar and his Senate must redress?" (p. 36) Clearly, Caesar considers Rome and the Senate to belong to him. In his exchange with the conspirators, Caesar will not reconsider his decision banishing Publius Cimber. He says he is incapable of making mistakes. "Know, Caesar doth not wrong." (p. 36) He considers himself no "ordinary man" and he can not be swayed by flattery.

However, Caesar's assessment of himself is not very accurate. He has already made some serious mistakes by dismissing the many warnings he has received, and by thinking the people around him are his friends. Also, Decius was able to flatter Caesar into changing his mind about coming to the Senate. Nevertheless, he says to Cassius, "I could be well moved, if I were as you; / If I could pray to move, prayers would move me: / But I am constant as the northern star." (p. 37) He says that trying to change Caesar's mind is an impossibility, like trying to lift Mount Olympus. The concern Brutus had in his garden about Caesar seems to be justified by Caesar's inflexibility.

Casca is the first to stab Caesar. It is fitting that Brutus be the last. Caesar's words to him—*Et tu Brutè?* (and thou, Brutus?)—indicate his disbelief that his friend could do such a thing.

In the panic that follows Caesar's death, Metellus warns the conspirators to "Stand fast together." (p. 38) But Brutus takes charge and assures the frightened senators that "Ambition's debt is paid." (p. 38) To mark themselves as the men who killed Caesar and gave their country "Liberty, freedom and enfranchisement," (p. 37) Brutus tells them to bathe their hands in Caesar's blood. With this act Calphurnia's dream comes true. Brutus is so blinded by delusions of his own nobility that he goes so far as to suggest that the conspirators have done Caesar a favor by killing him: "...then is death a benefit / So we are Caesar's friends, that have abridged / his time of fearing death." (p. 38)

The arrival of Antony provides another opportunity to study the differences between the idealistic Brutus and the practical Cassius. Brutus is innocent, to the point of being naive. Because he believes his motives for killing Caesar are noble and pure, and because any reasonable Roman would recognize them as such, Brutus has no problem with Antony's request to speak at Caesar's funeral. Since they all acted for the good of Rome, how could Antony, or any Roman, not understand? Cassius however, instinctively sees the political truth and knows the problems Antony may cause them. His strenuous objections are downplayed by Brutus, who thinks he can allay Cassius' fears by imposing restrictions on Antony. He tells Antony, "You shall not in your funeral speech blame us / But speak all good you can devise of Caesar / And say you do't by our permission; / …And you shall speak / In the same pulpit whereto I am going, / After my speech is ended." (p. 42)

When the others leave, the bloody Antony, who has shaken hands with each of the conspirators, indicates his true intentions in a soliloquy. He vows revenge for Caesar's murder, and he promises to throw Italy into such a violent civil war, "That mothers shall but smile when they behold / Their infants quarter'd with the hands of war; / All pity choked with custom of fell deeds." (p. 43)

The arrival of a messenger at the end of the scene introduces Octavius, Caesar's young nephew, who has an important role in the rest of the play.

Study Questions

1. Why does Caesar not read Artemidorus' letter?

2. Why does Cassius think their assassination plan has been discovered?

3. Why does Caesar get angry at Metellus?

4. What does Brutus tell the frightened senators after Caesar's assassination?

5. How does Calphurnia's dream come true?

6. What does Antony want from the conspirators?

7. What restrictions does Brutus place on Antony when he allows him to speak at the funeral?

8. What does Antony predict in his soliloquy?

9. What information does the messenger bring to Antony?

10. What are Antony's intentions as the scene ends?

Answers

1. He says because it is personal business it can wait. He puts affairs of state before personal matters.

2. Popilius Lena wishes him good luck in their enterprise and then he goes and talks to Caesar.

3. He thinks Metellus is trying to flatter him into changing his mind. Caesar says he cannot be swayed.

4. He says no harm is intended toward anyone else and they shouldn't be afraid.

5. Brutus tells the conspirators to bathe their hands and swords in Caesar's blood to mark them as the men who killed Caesar and gave their country freedom.

6. First he says he wants to die by Caesar if they intend to kill him. Then when he realizes he will be allowed to live, he wants to know why Caesar was killed and to speak at Caesar's funeral.

7. Antony may not blame the conspirators for killing Caesar, though he may say good things about Caesar. He must say he speaks by their permission. He must speak from the same place as Brutus after Brutus has first addressed the crowd.

8. He predicts a bloody civil war, with dead bodies waiting for burial, and revenge for Caesar's death.

9. Octavius, summoned by Caesar, has arrived outside of Rome.

10. He plans to stir up the crowd and then send word to Octavius if it is safe for him to enter Rome.

Suggested Essay Topics

1. A soliloquy is an important device to expose information and give the reader insight into a character. In a soliloquy, the character speaks the truth. Read Antony's soliloquy in this scene again. What truth does it reveal about Antony who has just apparently reconciled with the men who killed his friend, Caesar?

2. How does Caesar's "tragic flaw" of pride and ambition enable the events in this scene to occur? How could these events have been prevented?

Act III, Scenes II–III (pages 44–52)

New Characters:

Plebeians: *Roman citizens at Caesar's funeral*

Servant: *messenger from Octavius*

Cinna the Poet: *a poet with the same name as one of the conspirators*

Summary

The setting is in the marketplace at Caesar's funeral shortly after his death. The agitated crowd demands an explanation for Caesar's assassination. Cassius leaves with some of the crowd to give his version of why Caesar was killed, while Brutus remains behind with the others to give his own account of the events. Brutus explains that although he was Caesar's friend, and loved him, Caesar was ambitious and had to be killed for the good of Rome. If allowed to live, Caesar would have made slaves of all the Romans. He tells the crowd that he is ready to kill himself with the same dagger he used to kill Caesar, if they think he did wrong. But they are so moved by his speech that the crowd wants to erect statues in Brutus' honor and make him king. Brutus declines their offer, and after telling them to listen to what Antony has to say, Brutus leaves.

Antony faces a hostile audience when he ascends into the pulpit and begins his oration with the words, "Friends, Romans, countrymen, lend me your ears." (Sc. II, p. 46) Slowly he wins them over, proving that Caesar was not ambitious. He calls the conspirators "honorable men," yet he shows them to be traitors. Antony cries for Caesar and produces his will. He tells the angry citizens that he dare not read the will because it might stir them to mutiny and rage against Cassius and Brutus. He shows them Caesar's bloody cloak and his mutilated body, stirring them up with every word. And when he finally reads the will, revealing the generous legacy Caesar left the citizens of Rome, the crowd is transformed into an angry mob, out of control and intent on revenge against the conspirators. Antony is quite pleased with these results, and with the news brought by a messenger from Octavius, that Cassius and Brutus have fled Rome.

In the next scene, Cinna, the poet, on his way to Caesar's funeral, is confronted by a mob carrying torches and clubs. They demand answers to their questions, and when Cinna tells them his name they threaten to kill him as a conspirator. He says he isn't one of the conspirators, but a poet. The angry mob kills him anyway, "for his bad verses," (Sc. III, p. 52) and then runs off to burn the houses of the conspirators.

Analysis

The scene provides another example of subjective interpretation, and shows how it affects the actions of others. The crowd of citizens is moved first by Brutus' picture of Caesar, and then turned into an angry mob by a totally different Caesar painted by Antony. The fickleness of the Roman people, evident from the first scene of the play, becomes more apparent now. After Caesar's assassination, the angry crowd, commoners who were the foundation of Caesar's power, demand an explanation from the bloody men who just murdered their hero. Brutus is so sure killing Caesar was the right thing to do that he is ready to die for his convictions. He is so convincing in arguing that Caesar's ambition would have destroyed the Roman Republic that the crowd is eager to "Bring him with triumph home unto his house. / Give him a statue with his ancestors. / Let him be Caesar." (Sc. II, p. 45) In their response lies the irony. Brutus killed Caesar, who would be king, to deliver Rome from tyranny, and these same people would make their liberator king. They have missed the point behind Brutus' actions and oration.

Antony's funeral speech is the dramatic high point of the play. Not only is he able to stir up the Romans into a frenzied mob, as he predicted he would in his soliloquy in Act III, but he does so while fulfilling the restrictions imposed on him by Brutus. Antony cautiously ascends to the same pulpit as Brutus, after Brutus speaks, and he says he speaks by permission. He doesn't blame the conspirators, but uses the phrase "honorable men" with such unmistakable irony that the crowd calls them villains and murderers. His pun, "O judgement! thou art fled to brutish beasts," (Sc. II, p. 47) followed by his tears, has an electrifying effect on his audience. Antony manipulates the crowd by showing them Caesar's will, and then telling them he cannot read it. He holds off their demands to read it, allowing their emotions to build. Next, Antony, who was not present when Caesar was killed, shows them Caesar's cloak, and dramatically points out where each of the conspirators stabb'd. "Look, in this place ran Cassius' dagger through. / See what a rent the envious Casca made. / Through this the well-beloved Brutus stabb'd." (Sc. II, p. 49) It is a theatrical ploy, but most effective. The crowd even forgets about the will, until Antony reminds them. He reads the will: "To every Roman citizen he gives, / To every several man, seventy-five drachmas (silver coins)." (Sc. II, p. 51) And, "Moreover, he hath left you all his walks, / His private arbours, and new-planted orchards, / On this side Tiber." (Sc. II, p. 51) This pushes the crowd into a frenzy that Antony sets loose on Rome.

In a move of tactical brilliance, Antony announces himself as a lamb so he can later pounce like a lion:

> I come not, friends, to steal away your hearts
> I am no orator, as Brutus is;
> But, as you know me all, a plain blunt man,
> That love my friend; and that they know full well
> That gave me public leave to speak of him:
> For I have neither wit, nor words, nor worth,
> Action, nor utterance, nor the power of speech,
> To stir men's blood: I only speak right on. (Sc. II, p. 50)

By creating the illusion that he will not attempt to stir the crowd, he lowers its resistance, opens its heart, and firmly sinks in his teeth. In such a way, Antony easily manipulates the crowd, by claiming he is not the manipulative type. Furthermore, Antony cleverly attributes his own powers of manipulation to the unwitting Brutus by suggesting that he is not an orator like Brutus. Antony's political cunning is obvious, especially in contrast to Brutus' sincerity (albeit misguided).

Cinna, the poet, becomes the first victim of the mob. He is in the wrong place at the wrong time, drawn there by some unknown, supernatural forces. "I dreamt to-night that I did feast with Caesar, / And things unluckily charge my fantasy: / I have no will to wander forth of doors, / Yet something leads me forth." (Sc. III, I–IV, p. 52) He is surrounded by people out for revenge, who ask him many questions but are not interested in his answers. He responds to one of these questions about being married or single, "Wisely I say, I am a bachelor." (Sc. III, p. 52) They then threaten to beat him for implying "they are fools that marry." (Sc. III, p. 52) Clearly the mob is out for blood. Ultimately they kill him just for being there, using his "bad verses" as their justification.

Act III ends with Rome in complete chaos and on the brink of civil war.

Study Questions

1. How does Brutus justify the killing of Caesar to the people of Rome?

2. What is the crowd's reaction to Brutus' speech?

3. What two reasons does Antony give to prove Caesar wasn't ambitious?

4. How does Antony use irony in his funeral speech?

5. What is the pun Antony uses in this line from Scene II: "O judgement! thou art fled to brutish beasts," (p. 47)?

6. How does Antony use Caesar's cloak to manipulate the crowd?

7. How does Antony say that Caesar died?

8. What is the news that the messenger brings to Antony at the end of the scene?

9. Why is Cinna out on the streets?

10. What is the excuse the mob uses to kill Cinna?

Answers

1. Caesar was ambitious and Brutus says he killed him because he loved Rome more than Caesar.

2. They want to erect statues in his honor and make him king.

3. Caesar was too sensitive and cried when he saw the poor crying. "Ambition should be made of sterner stuff." (Sc. II, p. 47) Also, Caesar refused the crown three times when Antony offered it to him on the feast of Lupercal.

4. He uses the words "honorable men" repeatedly, twisting the meaning so the crowd understands that he means the exact opposite.

5. He uses the phrase "brutish beasts," a pun on Brutus' name and his bestial behavior in killing Caesar.

6. He points out the rips in the cloak and describes where each of the conspirators stabbed Caesar, even though he wasn't there to witness the event.

7. He says that Caesar died of a broken heart when he was stabbed by Brutus who was Caesar's angel (best friend).

8. Octavius is outside of Rome, and Brutus and Cassius have fled the city.

9. He is on his way to Caesar's funeral, driven out of doors by some unknown force.

10. They kill him for writing bad poetry.

Suggested Essay Topics

1. Compare the funeral speeches of Brutus and Antony. What are their purposes? How effective is each speech? How does each speech reveal important aspects of both characters?

2. The fickleness of the crowd is an important issue in the play. Brutus and Antony both depend on it. How are they able to manipulate the crowd in this scene? What other devices do they use in their funeral speeches to win the support of the crowd? Which speech is more effective and why? Give reasons for your opinions.

SECTION FIVE

Act IV

Act IV, Scene I (pages 53–54)

New Characters:

Octavius: *Caesar's nephew and one of the three leaders to rule Rome after his death*

Lepidus: *the third leader to rule Rome after Caesar's death*

Summary

The setting is a house in Rome some time after Caesar's death. The Republic is in turmoil, as Antony predicted. Rome is in the hands of Antony, Octavius, and Lepidus. They are compiling a death list of their political enemies. Antony sends Lepidus to "fetch" Caesar's will so they might reduce some of the legacies mentioned by Antony to the citizens in his funeral speech. When Lepidus leaves, Antony tells Octavius that Lepidus is unfit to have so much power. Antony plans to use Lepidus to achieve his political objectives and then cut him off. They talk about Brutus and Cassius, who have fled the country and are raising an army in Greece. Antony and Octavius make plans to muster their own forces to fight them.

Analysis

Act IV addresses the corrupting effects of power. Rome is on the brink of a terrible civil war. Antony has joined forces with Octavius and Lepidus to become one of the three most powerful men in Rome. They are the second triumvirate to rule the Republic. (Caesar, Pompey, and Crassus were the first.)

To solidify their political power, and because they have many enemies in Rome, they are making a list of Roman senators and citizens they plan to execute. Their decisions are cold and unfeeling. In a political tit-for-tat, Lepidus consents to listing his own brother, provided that Antony agrees to include his nephew. Ironically, their total disregard for life goes beyond anything Brutus feared Caesar might do. Their greed is made more evident in their plan to change Caesar's will for their personal gain.

The moral flaw in Antony's character can also be seen when he reveals his contempt for Lepidus. When Octavius calls Lepidus "a tried and valiant soldier," (p. 54) Antony compares Lepidus to his horse who "must be taught and train'd and bid go forth." (p. 54) It is Antony's intention to use Lepidus as a practical means to his desired end, much as Cassius used Brutus. It is not a flattering picture of the man who rose to great heights in Act III, and who is about to lead Rome into civil war.

Study Questions

1. Why are Antony, Octavius, and Lepidus together in the scene?
2. How does Shakespeare show their callousness?
3. Why does Antony send Lepidus to Caesar's house?
4. What is Antony's true opinion of Lepidus?
5. Why did Antony pick Lepidus as one of the new leaders of Rome?
6. What does Antony compare Lepidus to?
7. What is Octavius' assessment of Lepidus?
8. What is Antony's response to Octavius?
9. What news does Antony tell Octavius about Brutus and Cassius?
10. Why does Octavius agree with Antony's plan to go after Cassius and Brutus?

Answers

1. They are making a list of people to be killed in order to tighten their control in Rome.

2. Lepidus agrees to have his brother placed on the list if Antony agrees to condemn his own nephew.

3. He sends him for Caesar's will. They plan to reduce what Caesar left to the Roman citizens.

4. He thinks Lepidus is fit to be sent on errands, but not fit to be one of the three most powerful men in the world.

5. Antony needs Lepidus to gain favorable public opinion.

6. He compares him to a mule that carries a load from one place to another and then is turned loose to graze. He also compares him to his horse.

7. Octavius says Lepidus is an experienced and brave soldier.

8. Antony says his horse is also a brave soldier, who must be taught to fight, run, and stop, and be ruled by Antony, as must Lepidus.

9. They are raising an army in Greece and preparing for war.

10. He says they are surrounded by many enemies in Rome and those who pretend to be their friends are not.

Suggested Essay Topics

1. What does this scene reveal about Octavius? What new insight does it give into Antony's character, and how does that effect your opinion of him?

2. Antony and Octavius will become the focus of attention for the remainder of the play and Shakespeare will write about them again in *Antony and Cleopatra*. Little is said or known of Lepidus. Research the life of Lepidus. What is his background? Where did he come from, and what happened to him after the civil war with Brutus and Cassius?

Act IV, Scenes II–III (pages 55–66)

New Characters:

Pindarus: *servant to Cassius taken prisoner in Partheia*

Lucilius: *officer in Brutus' army*

Messala: *officer in Brutus' army*

Titinius: *friend of Cassius and Officer in his army*

Varro: *soldier in Brutus' army*

Claudius: *soldier in Brutus' army*

Poet: *jester who enters Brutus' tent*

Caesar's Ghost

Soldiers

Summary

The setting is the camp of Brutus in Sardis, Greece. Brutus and his soldiers are awaiting the arrival of Cassius and his army. When Pindarus, a slave to Cassius, brings his master's greetings, Brutus indicates his misgivings about the course of events. He confides to Lucilius, one of his officers, that he has regrets about killing Caesar.

As soon as Cassius arrives in camp he begins to quarrel with Brutus. Brutus cautions him that they should not fight in front of the troops they will soon lead into battle, so they move into Brutus' tent to continue their argument.

Cassius is angry because a friend of his, Lucius Pella, has been punished for taking bribes and Brutus ignored letters that Cassius wrote in the man's defense. Brutus attacks Cassius for defending Pella, and he attacks Cassius' own reputation for taking bribes. As their tempers flare, they come to the point of drawing swords. Cassius physically threatens Brutus, who dismisses him as a "slight man," (Sc. III, p. 58) and reminds him that they killed Caesar for the sake of justice and not for personal gain.

Brutus is angry because he sent a request to Cassius for money to pay his troops and Cassius refused. Cassius denies refusing the money, and is so disturbed by what Brutus thinks that he offers him his dagger and tells Brutus to kill him. This calms Brutus and he and Cassius shake hands, reaffirming their friendship. Brutus tells Cassius he is distraught because he learned of his wife's death in letters from Rome. Depressed by Brutus' flight, she committed suicide.

Messala and Titinius, officers in their armies, enter with news from Rome, confirming Portia's death, along with the murder of 70 to 100 Roman senators.

Brutus turns their attention back to "our work alive," a battle plan to meet the advancing enemy armies. Brutus wants to march to Philippi, while Cassius thinks they should remain where they are and have their enemies come to them. Brutus argues that they are in unfriendly territory, at the peak of their strength, and they must seize the opportunity before they weaken. Once again Cassius gives in to Brutus, and the decision is made to set off for Philippi in the morning.

While reading a book in his tent Brutus begins to doze. In this twilight of consciousness, the ghost of Caesar appears to him. The ghost says he is Brutus' evil spirit, and that he will see Brutus again at Philippi. Before Brutus awakens fully the ghost is gone. Brutus calls Varro and Claudius, soldiers in his army, and tells them to send word to Cassius to move his troops to Philippi at once.

Analysis

As Scene I showed the corrupting effects of power on Antony, Octavius, and Lepidus, these scenes indicate the breakdown in the relationship between Brutus and Cassius. The passage of time, the unexpected chaos that has developed in Rome, the reaction of the Roman people, and Cassius' behavior have made Brutus wish "Things done undone." (Sc. II, p. 55) Nothing is what he expected.

His meeting with Cassius in the camp at Sardis is a confrontation over money, but there are deeper issues addressed during their fight in the tent. Cassius is angry because he thinks Brutus wronged him when he disregarded the letters Cassius wrote in defense of Lucius Pella. Brutus, however, thinks that Cassius wronged himself to sanction bribery. He questions Cassius' honesty and accuses him of taking bribes and selling his favors to the highest bidder. Cassius is infuriated, but Brutus, whose motives are always noble, reminds Cassius that they killed Caesar for justice, not for money.

Cassius warns Brutus not to bait him or he may do something he will be sorry for. Brutus responds, "You have done that you should be sorry for," (Sc. III, p. 59) meaning the assassination of Caesar. At the point of drawing their swords, Brutus tells Cassius he is not afraid of him. "There is no terror, Cassius, in your threats; / For I am arm'd so strong in honesty, / That they pass by me as the idle wind / Which I respect not." (Sc. III, p. 59) He confronts Cassius with the fact that when Brutus needed money to pay his army, Cassius refused to send it to him.

Cassius is so troubled by what Brutus says that he calls upon Antony and Octavius to come and avenge themselves on Cassius. Then Cassius offers Brutus his sword and tells him to use it on him:

> There is my dagger,
> And here my naked breast; within, a heart
> Dearer than Plutus' mine, richer than gold:
> If thou be'st a Roman, take it forth;
> I, that denied thee gold, will give my heart:
> Strike, as thou didst at Caesar; for I know,
> When thou didst hate him worst, thou lovedst him better
> Than ever thou lovedst Cassius. (Sc. III, p. 60)

His words calm Brutus and they shake hands and make up. It is then that Brutus tells Cassius about the unusual circumstances of Portia's death. She committed suicide by swallowing burning coals.

Titinius and Messala arrive to make plans for battle. Messala confirms the deaths of Portia and 70–100 senators, including Cicero. They are the casualties of the death list compiled by Antony, Octavius, and Lepidus earlier.

The rest of the scene serves to show that Brutus is still making the decisions. Despite the objections of Cassius, Brutus convinces them it would be better to march to Philippi. The Sardians become Brutus' soldiers due to forced loyalty, and thus, may join the enemy. Brutus says it would be safer to put the Sardians at their backs and march out to meet the enemy. He uses a sea metaphor to make his point:

> There is a tide in the affairs of men
> Which taken at the flood leads on to fortune;
> Omitted, all the voyage of their life
> Is bound in shallows and in miseries.
> On such a full sea are we now afloat,
> And we must take the current when it serves,
> Or lose our ventures. (Sc. III, p. 63)

Throughout the play Brutus has made serious errors in judgment in letting Antony live, and allowing him to speak at Caesar's funeral. It is the decision to march to Philippi however, that will prove to be a fatal mistake for Cassius and Brutus.

The scene ends with another appearance of the supernatural, a visit from Caesar's ghost, as Antony predicted earlier in his soliloquy in Act III. But is it really Caesar's spirit Brutus sees as he dozes over a book, or Brutus having qualms of conscience for what he has done? The apparition foreshadows Philippi, where Brutus will see Caesar's ghost again.

Study Questions

1. Why is Brutus concerned about Lucilius' account of his meeting with Cassius?

2. Why does Brutus tell Cassius to come into his tent?

3. Why is Cassius angry with Brutus?

4. Why is Brutus angry with Cassius?

5. Why does Brutus say he is not afraid of Cassius' threats?

6. What is the advice given to Cassius and Brutus by the poet?

7. What is the news from Rome?

8. What are Brutus' and Cassius' battle plans?

9. What reasons does Brutus give for his plan?

10. What does the ghost of Caesar tell Brutus?

Answers

1. It reaffirms Brutus' feelings that Cassius' friendship seems to be cooling down.

2. He doesn't want their troops to see them fighting.

3. Brutus disregarded letters Cassius wrote in defense of Lucius Pella, who was accused of taking bribes.

4. Brutus sent to Cassius for money to pay his soldiers and his request was denied.

5. Brutus says he is so honest that Cassius' threats mean nothing and pass him by like the idle wind.

6. He tells them to "Love, and be friends, as two such men should be." (Sc. III, p. 61)

7. Between 70 and 100 senators, including Cicero, have been killed by Antony, Octavius, and Lepidus. Portia committed suicide by swallowing fire.

8. Brutus wants to march their armies from Sardis to Philippi and meet the enemy there. Cassius wants to remain where they are and have the enemy come to them.

9. He says the Sardians are not friendly. Their armies are at peak strength, and if they delay they will weaken. He says the opportunity to act is at hand, and if they do not take it, they will miss their chance for success.

10. The ghost says it is Brutus' evil spirit, and that it will see Brutus again at Philippi.

Suggested Essay Topics

1. Critics have said that Caesar has a stronger influence on the events, the outcome, and the characters in the play after his death than he did when he was living. Explain why you agree or disagree with this, and give reasons to support your opinions.

2. The critic G. Wilson Knight has described the importance of sleep in *Julius Caesar*. Sleep is mentioned by Brutus in his soliloquy in the first scene of Act II. It is brought up by Portia, and Calphurnia's dream is very significant. Discuss the sleep imagery in the play and show how it is important.

SECTION SIX

Act V

Act V, Scene I (pages 67–71)

Summary

The setting is on the battlefield at Philippi. Antony and Octavius, at the head of their armies, are preparing to begin the battle. Through spies Antony knows the enemy is not ready for the fight. A messenger brings word that the battle is at hand. Before the combat, Antony and Octavius go into the field to exchange insults with Brutus and Cassius. They call each other traitors to Rome. Cassius says to Brutus that Antony would not be alive if Cassius had his way on the ides of March. They break off and plan to settle matters with their swords.

Cassius confides in Messala that he is reluctant to fight this battle on his birthday. He has seen signs that have convinced him that they are going to lose. But he is resigned to face whatever comes. Cassius and Brutus discuss what they will do if they are defeated. Both agree that they will not be led as captives back to Rome. Although Brutus is opposed to suicide, he will die before he is taken prisoner. They say their final good-byes and prepare for the battle.

Analysis

The battle to decide the fate of Rome is at hand. The growing conflict between Antony and young Octavius is foreshadowed by their exchange prior to the battle. Antony tries to tell Octavius to fight on the left side of the field, but Octavius asserts himself and refuses to be ordered by Antony. When Antony asks him why he opposes him, Octavius responds, "I do not cross you; but I will do so." (p. 68)

In the play the four generals never face one another in a decisive battle or even a fight. Instead, their confrontation is one of words, insults, and accusations, before the war begins. When Antony attacks Brutus and Cassius as villains and flatterers, Cassius takes the opportunity to tell Brutus, "I told you so." "Now, Brutus, thank yourself:/ This tongue had not offended so to-day, / If Cassius might have ruled." (p. 68) His instincts about Antony are proven to be correct.

Superstition manifests itself again in this scene, as Cassius tells Messala that although he "held Epicurus strong" (did not believe in the supernatural influence on human affairs) he knows they are going to lose the battle because of the omens he has observed. The mighty eagles once perched on their battle ensigns, fed by his soldiers, have been replaced by ravens, crows and kites, scavengers that feast on corpses and "Fly o'er our heads and downward look on us, / As we were sickly prey." (p. 70)

The farewell between Brutus and Cassius is the last time Brutus will see his brother-in-law alive. Time is running out for both of them. Cassius speaks of the worst case scenario, and both agree that they will kill themselves rather than face defeat at the hands of Antony and Octavius. But win or lose, Brutus is content that whatever the outcome of the day's events, it will end what began on the ides of March.

Study Questions

1. What does Octavius report to Antony in the opening lines of the scene?

2. What is the cause of the disagreement between Antony and Octavius?

3. How does Antony insult Cassius and Brutus?

4. What is Cassius' response to Antony's insult?

5. Why is Cassius reluctant to fight the battle?

6. What are the omens he has observed?

7. Why would it be ironic if Cassius dies in the battle?

8. What is Brutus' attitude concerning suicide?

9. What is Brutus' response when Cassius asks if he is "contented to be led in triumph / Thorough the streets of Rome?" (p. 70)

10. Why is Brutus anxious for the battle to begin?

Answers

1. The enemy is preparing to attack before Antony and Octavius are ready.

2. Antony tells Octavius to fight on the left side of the field, but Octavius says no.

3. He calls them villains and flatterers.

4. Cassius tells Brutus he should have listened to him and killed Antony when they killed Caesar.

5. From the signs and omens he is sure they will lose.

6. The eagles that were perched on their battle flags flew away and were replaced by ravens, crows, and kites, birds that feed on dead bodies.

7. It is his birthday.

8. He condemned his father-in-law, Cato, for killing himself rather than live under Caesar. He thinks it cowardly and vile to commit suicide in fear of what may happen in the future.

9. Brutus says he will never go back to Rome as a prisoner.

10. Win or lose, he wants to end the work that began on the ides of March.

Suggested Essay Topics

1. In literature the *climax* is defined as the highest point of action in a story, where the conflict is resolved. The battle between Cassius and Brutus and Antony and Octavius would seem to be the climax of the play, but this confrontation

never takes place. When do you think the climax of the play occurs? Give reasons for your opinions.

2. Write a character sketch of Brutus, Cassius, Antony, Octavius and Caesar based on their actions, what they say, and what others say about them. What are their strong points and their weaknesses? Which character is the most interesting in your opinion and why?

Act V, Scenes II–III (pages 71–75)

New Character:

Cato: *Brutus' brother-in-law and a soldier in his army*

Summary

The battle begins as Brutus orders Messala to send all of his legions against Octavius' army. While Brutus gains the advantage on another part of the field, Cassius is in retreat, surrounded by Antony's forces. Pindarus, the slave of Cassius, enters with a warning for his master to fall back further. But Cassius decides that he has retreated far enough. He asks his friend, Titinius, to ride his horse and determine if the soldiers in his tents are friend or enemy. As Pindarus climbs the hill to report Titinius' progress, Cassius considers the real possibility that his life has reached its end on his birthday. Pindarus describes Titinius overtaken and surrounded by horsemen, and as Titinius dismounts, he is captured by the cheering soldiers.

Cassius, ashamed that he has lived to see his best friend taken by the enemy, promises to give Pindarus his freedom in exchange for Pindarus ending Cassius' life by stabbing him.

After Cassius' death Pindarus runs from the battlefield, and Titinius, holding a wreath of flowers, returns with Messala and the news of Brutus' victory. They discover the body of Cassius and Messala leaves to tell Brutus the bad news. When Titinius is alone with Cassius' body, he places the wreath on Cassius' head and then he kills himself with Cassius' sword, as a final act of loyalty to his friend.

When Brutus enters with young Cato and Messala, they find two dead bodies to be mourned. Brutus says that the carnage is

the spirit of Caesar, who is "mighty yet...and turns our swords /
In our own proper entrails." (Sc. III, p. 74)

Since the first fight was not decisive—Cassius was defeated by
Antony, while Octavius was defeated by Brutus—preparations are
made for the final battle.

Analysis

Throughout the play Brutus has been the noble hero, who has
made errors only because of his honesty, moral principles, or political naivete. In this scene Cassius, perhaps the least noble of the
main characters in he play, rises in stature. Here, however, he makes
the one mistake that will prove fatal. His army is in retreat and on
the verge of mutiny. They are surrounded by Antony, when Brutus'
troops, gaining the advantage over Octavius, stop fighting to loot the
dead bodies instead of supporting Cassius' army. When Pindarus,
the slave Cassius captured years before in Parthia, announces, "Mark
Antony is in your tents, my lord: / Fly, therefore, noble Cassius, fly
far off," (Sc. III, p. 72) the "noble" Cassius is determined to make his
stand and not retreat. When Cassius asks his friend Titinius to take
his horse and ride down to see who is in his tents, Titinius indicates
his love, honor, and respect for Cassius by his quick actions. He is
ready and willing to put his own life on the line for his friend. "I will
be here again, even with a thought." (Sc. III, p. 72)

Cassius' fatal error comes when he infers from Pindarus' account that Titinius was captured by enemy troops. It is another
example of how subjective interpretation effects the actions of
another. True to his word, Cassius makes good on his pledge to Brutus to commit suicide rather than surrender. He calls on Pindarus
to return the kindness Cassius once showed him. When Pindarus
was captured in battle, Cassius spared his life, evoking a promise
from him to do whatever Cassius asked of him. Now Cassius grants
Pindarus his freedom in exchange for stabbing him when his head
is turned. It is Pindarus' words that express his feelings. He would
rather Cassius be alive and remain his slave. "So, I am free; yet
would not so have been, / Durst I have done my will. O Cassius!"
(Sc. III, p.73)

The arrival of Titinius and Messala provides an explanation of
the events misinterpreted by Cassius. The troops that surrounded

Titinius were Brutus' men. Their shout was one of joy. The garland Titinius carries, to be presented to Cassius, is a token of Brutus' victory over Octavius.

Titinius shows his love for Cassius by his words and his actions. After sending Messala to bring the bad news to Brutus, Titinius kills himself with Cassius' sword. His final words are a tribute to his friend. "Brutus, come apace, / And see how I regarded Caius Cassius. / By your leave, gods: this is a Roman's part: / Come, Cassius' sword, and find Titinius' heart." (Sc. III, p. 74)

Brutus' reaction to their deaths is one of sorrow and tribute. He calls them "the last of all the Romans" (Sc. III, p. 74) and says that Rome can never again produce such a breed. Although Cassius is not the tragic hero of the play, in death he has grown in stature.

The scene ends with Cassius' body being sent to Thasos, a Greek island in the Aegean, to await funeral rites, as Brutus readies his troops to "try fortune in a second fight." (Sc. III, p. 75)

Study Questions

1. What order does Brutus give Messala in the battle?
2. How does Cassius try to prevent the retreat?
3. What news does Pindarus bring the retreating Cassius?
4. Why does Cassius ask Pindarus to describe Titinius' ride instead of doing so himself?
5. What does Pindarus describe?
6. What request does Cassius make of Pindarus?
7. What is ironic about the way Cassius dies?
8. What is the message Titinius has for Cassius?
9. How does Titinius show his high regard for Cassius?
10. Why does Brutus plan to send Cassius' body to Thasos for burial?

Answers

1. Brutus tells him to ride and order his army to attack Octavius' flank (wing).

2. He killed his own ensign (flag carrier) when the soldier retreated, causing Cassius' troops to follow the flag.

3. Antony's troops are in Cassius' tents.

4. He says that he has bad eyesight.

5. Titinius is surrounded. He is taken and the soldiers shout for joy at his capture.

6. He asks Pindarus to kill him in exchange for his freedom.

7. He is killed on his birthday by the same sword that killed Caesar.

8. Brutus has won his battle, and he brings a wreath of victory to present to Cassius.

9. He kills himself with Cassius' sword.

10. He doesn't want his army to become depressed because of Cassius' death as they plan for the final battle.

Suggested Essay Topics

1. Caesar considered Cassius a threat, a dangerous man who thought too much. Brutus called his brother-in-law "the last of all the Romans." Research the life of Cassius. Whose evaluation of Cassius is closer to the truth? Who is the real Cassius?

2. Who do you think makes a better leader, a pragmatist (a practical, political person like Cassius) or an idealist (a man of principle such as Brutus)? Can a leader ever be both? Support your conclusions with specific references to the events of the play.

Act V, Scenes IV and V (pages 75–78)

New Characters:

Clitus, Dardanus, Strato, and Volumnius: *soldiers in Brutus' army*

Summary

At the height of the second battle Brutus charges into the field. Young Cato is killed and Lucilius, an officer in Brutus' army, is captured. To confuse the enemy soldiers, Lucilius tells them he is Brutus, and offers them money to kill him. Antony identifies their captive and tells the soldiers to keep Lucilius safely under guard.

On another part of the field, after hours of fighting, Brutus and his men are in retreat. They have lost the war. Brutus begs Clitus, Volumnius, and Dardanus to assist him in his suicide, but they decline and run off as Antony and Octavius advance. Brutus convinces Strato to hold his sword while Brutus runs onto it and kills himself.

Octavius and Antony arrive with Lucilius and Messala under guard. When they ask for Brutus, Strato says his master is safe from capture and humiliation. Octavius offers amnesty for those who served Brutus and takes them into his army, restoring order after the chaos of civil war. Antony praises Brutus, calling him a noble Roman and an honest man, the best of the conspirators. The play ends with Octavius making plans to bury the dead, including Brutus, who will be given an honorable soldier's burial, and spread the news of their great victory.

Analysis

The end arrives as Brutus sees his soldiers and his friends killed or captured. Lucilius is taken by Antony's soldiers. He tries to confuse them by claiming that he is Brutus, to allow the real Brutus to escape. But Antony recognizes him and tells his soldiers, "Give him all kindness: I had rather have / Such men my friends than enemies." (Sc. IV, p. 76) Antony seems to be recruiting allies for a future clash with Octavius.

Brutus now realizes he has lost. "Our enemies have beat us to the pit: / It is more worthy to leap in ourselves / Than tarry till they push us." (Sc. V, p. 77) Brutus is in tears when he pleads for someone to assist him in his plan to kill himself, but Clitus, Dardanus and Volumnius turn down his request as "not an office for a friend, my lord." (Sc. V, p. 77)

Brutus says his final farewells, content that he is going to his death knowing that what he did was right for Rome. He is still unaware that he was tricked into the conspiracy by Cassius. He tells his "poor remains of friends" "My heart doth joy that yet in all my life / I found no man but he was true to me." (Sc. V, p. 77) It is Strato who proves to be Brutus' best friend, agreeing to hold his sword while Brutus impales himself on the blade. His last words are addressed to Caesar's spirit. "Caesar, now be still:/ I kill'd not thee with half so good a will." (Sc. V, p. 78)

The arrival of Octavius and Antony gives the play closure and restores the world to its rightful order. By granting amnesty to the rebellious soldiers, Octavius ends the civil war that has torn Rome apart. A final peace is made with Brutus, the real tragic hero of the play. Antony honors Brutus and his reputation in death even though he attacked him in life before the battle. He calls him "the noblest Roman of them all." (Sc. V, p. 78) He recognizes that all of the others acted out of envy for Caesar, but Brutus acted for the common good. Antony says of Brutus something he might have said of Caesar in his funeral oration: "His life was gentle, and the elements / So mix'd in him that Nature might stand up / And say to all the world 'This was a man!'" (Sc. V, p 78)

With the final words from Octavius—the new Caesar—the Roman world is settled, at least for now, as the play ends.

Study Questions

1. What happens to young Cato?

2. How does Lucilius try to confuse the enemy troops?

3. What does Lucilius request of the two soldiers?

4. What does Antony do when he recognizes Lucilius?

5. Why does Brutus say he wants to commit suicide?

6. What is the one thing Brutus says he is happy about before he dies?

7. How does Brutus die?

8. How does Strato answer Messala's inquiry about Brutus?

9. How does Octavius restore order to Rome after the battle?

10. How does Antony regard Brutus at the end of the play?

Answers

1. He is killed in the battle.

2. Lucilius tells his capturers that he is Brutus.

3. He offers them money and asks them to kill him.

4. He tells his men to treat Lucilius well and keep him safe because he wants him as a friend.

5. He uses the metaphor of a pit. His enemies have forced them to the edge and it is more noble to jump in than be pushed in.

6. Brutus is happy that in all his life his friends have been truthful and honest with him. The irony is that he was tricked by Cassius into joining the conspiracy against Caesar.

7. Strato holds his sword and Brutus runs onto it, stabbing himself.

8. He tells him that Brutus is safe from bondage (captivity), and that he was not conquered by his enemy. Brutus only conquered himself.

9. He gives amnesty to those who fought on the side of Brutus, and he invites them into his army.

10. He calls him a noble Roman who did what he thought was right. He was the only one who acted against Caesar for unselfish reasons, the common good.

Suggested Essay Topics

1. Some critics contend the play should have been titled *Marcus Brutus* instead of *Julius Caesar* because he is the real tragic hero of the play. Discuss this idea in a short essay and give your reasons why you agree or disagree.

2. Caesar and Brutus had a great deal in common. Both men were misled and manipulated by their friends. Show how this is true in terms of what happens to each of them in the course of the play.

3. According to some critics, *Julius Caesar* is misinterpreted by modern audiences who are concerned with democracy and freedom. According to these critics, Shakespeare had a different view of things. He lived under a monarch in a time of peace and prosperity, after a series of bloody civil wars. To Shakespeare, Brutus was a villain in this play and not a hero. He murdered a popular ruler and destroyed the social order. Do you agree or disagree with this interpretation of the play? Provide evidence from the play to support your opinions.

FICTION

FLATLAND: A ROMANCE OF MANY DIMENSIONS, Edwin A. Abbott. (0-486-27263-X)

PRIDE AND PREJUDICE, Jane Austen. (0-486-28473-5)

CIVIL WAR SHORT STORIES AND POEMS, Edited by Bob Blaisdell. (0-486-48226-X)

THE DECAMERON: Selected Tales, Giovanni Boccaccio. Edited by Bob Blaisdell. (0-486-41113-3)

JANE EYRE, Charlotte Brontë. (0-486-42449-9)

WUTHERING HEIGHTS, Emily Brontë. (0-486-29256-8)

THE THIRTY-NINE STEPS, John Buchan. (0-486-28201-5)

ALICE'S ADVENTURES IN WONDERLAND, Lewis Carroll. (0-486-27543-4)

MY ÁNTONIA, Willa Cather. (0-486-28240-6)

THE AWAKENING, Kate Chopin. (0-486-27786-0)

HEART OF DARKNESS, Joseph Conrad. (0-486-26464-5)

LORD JIM, Joseph Conrad. (0-486-40650-4)

THE RED BADGE OF COURAGE, Stephen Crane. (0-486-26465-3)

THE WORLD'S GREATEST SHORT STORIES, Edited by James Daley. (0-486-44716-2)

A CHRISTMAS CAROL, Charles Dickens. (0-486-26865-9)

GREAT EXPECTATIONS, Charles Dickens. (0-486-41586-4)

A TALE OF TWO CITIES, Charles Dickens. (0-486-40651-2)

CRIME AND PUNISHMENT, Fyodor Dostoyevsky. Translated by Constance Garnett. (0-486-41587-2)

THE ADVENTURES OF SHERLOCK HOLMES, Sir Arthur Conan Doyle. (0-486-47491-7)

THE HOUND OF THE BASKERVILLES, Sir Arthur Conan Doyle. (0-486-28214-7)

BLAKE: PROPHET AGAINST EMPIRE, David V. Erdman. (0-486-26719-9)

WHERE ANGELS FEAR TO TREAD, E. M. Forster. (0-486-27791-7)

BEOWULF, Translated by R. K. Gordon. (0-486-27264-8)

THE RETURN OF THE NATIVE, Thomas Hardy. (0-486-43165-7)

THE SCARLET LETTER, Nathaniel Hawthorne. (0-486-28048-9)

SIDDHARTHA, Hermann Hesse. (0-486-40653-9)

THE ODYSSEY, Homer. (0-486-40654-7)

THE TURN OF THE SCREW, Henry James. (0-486-26684-2)

DUBLINERS, James Joyce. (0-486-26870-5)

FICTION

THE METAMORPHOSIS AND OTHER STORIES, Franz Kafka. (0-486-29030-1)

SONS AND LOVERS, D. H. Lawrence. (0-486-42121-X)

THE CALL OF THE WILD, Jack London. (0-486-26472-6)

GREAT AMERICAN SHORT STORIES, Edited by Paul Negri. (0-486-42119-8)

THE GOLD-BUG AND OTHER TALES, Edgar Allan Poe. (0-486-26875-6)

ANTHEM, Ayn Rand. (0-486-49277-X)

FRANKENSTEIN, Mary Shelley. (0-486-28211-2)

THE JUNGLE, Upton Sinclair. (0-486-41923-1)

THREE LIVES, Gertrude Stein. (0-486-28059-4)

THE STRANGE CASE OF DR. JEKYLL AND MR. HYDE, Robert Louis Stevenson. (0-486-26688-5)

DRACULA, Bram Stoker. (0-486-41109-5)

UNCLE TOM'S CABIN, Harriet Beecher Stowe. (0-486-44028-1)

ADVENTURES OF HUCKLEBERRY FINN, Mark Twain. (0-486-28061-6)

THE ADVENTURES OF TOM SAWYER, Mark Twain. (0-486-40077-8)

CANDIDE, Voltaire. Edited by Francois-Marie Arouet. (0-486-26689-3)

THE COUNTRY OF THE BLIND: and Other Science-Fiction Stories, H. G. Wells. Edited by Martin Gardner. (0-486-48289-8)

THE WAR OF THE WORLDS, H. G. Wells. (0-486-29506-0)

ETHAN FROME, Edith Wharton. (0-486-26690-7)

THE PICTURE OF DORIAN GRAY, Oscar Wilde. (0-486-27807-7)

MONDAY OR TUESDAY: Eight Stories, Virginia Woolf. (0-486-29453-6)

NONFICTION

POETICS, Aristotle. (0-486-29577-X)

MEDITATIONS, Marcus Aurelius. (0-486-29823-X)

THE WAY OF PERFECTION, St. Teresa of Avila. Edited and Translated by
E. Allison Peers. (0-486-48451-3)

THE DEVIL'S DICTIONARY, Ambrose Bierce. (0-486-27542-6)

GREAT SPEECHES OF THE 20TH CENTURY, Edited by Bob Blaisdell.
(0-486-47467-4)

THE COMMUNIST MANIFESTO AND OTHER REVOLUTIONARY WRITINGS:
Marx, Marat, Paine, Mao Tse-Tung, Gandhi and Others, Edited by Bob Blaisdell.
(0-486-42465-0)

INFAMOUS SPEECHES: From Robespierre to Osama bin Laden, Edited by Bob
Blaisdell. (0-486-47849-1)

GREAT ENGLISH ESSAYS: From Bacon to Chesterton, Edited by Bob Blaisdell.
(0-486-44082-6)

GREEK AND ROMAN ORATORY, Edited by Bob Blaisdell. (0-486-49622-8)

THE UNITED STATES CONSTITUTION: The Full Text with Supplementary
Materials, Edited and with supplementary materials by Bob Blaisdell.
(0-486-47166-7)

GREAT SPEECHES BY NATIVE AMERICANS, Edited by Bob Blaisdell.
(0-486-41122-2)

GREAT SPEECHES BY AFRICAN AMERICANS: Frederick Douglass, Sojourner
Truth, Dr. Martin Luther King, Jr., Barack Obama, and Others, Edited by
James Daley. (0-486-44761-8)

GREAT SPEECHES BY AMERICAN WOMEN, Edited by James Daley.
(0-486-46141-6)

HISTORY'S GREATEST SPEECHES, Edited by James Daley. (0-486-49739-9)

GREAT INAUGURAL ADDRESSES, Edited by James Daley. (0-486-44577-1)

GREAT SPEECHES ON GAY RIGHTS, Edited by James Daley. (0-486-47512-3)

ON THE ORIGIN OF SPECIES: By Means of Natural Selection, Charles Darwin.
(0-486-45006-6)

NARRATIVE OF THE LIFE OF FREDERICK DOUGLASS, Frederick Douglass.
(0-486-28499-9)

THE SOULS OF BLACK FOLK, W. E. B. Du Bois. (0-486-28041-1)

NATURE AND OTHER ESSAYS, Ralph Waldo Emerson. (0-486-46947-6)

SELF-RELIANCE AND OTHER ESSAYS, Ralph Waldo Emerson. (0-486-27790-9)

THE LIFE OF OLAUDAH EQUIANO, Olaudah Equiano. (0-486-40661-X)

WIT AND WISDOM FROM POOR RICHARD'S ALMANACK, Benjamin Franklin.
(0-486-40891-4)

THE AUTOBIOGRAPHY OF BENJAMIN FRANKLIN, Benjamin Franklin.
(0-486-29073-5)

NONFICTION

THE DECLARATION OF INDEPENDENCE AND OTHER GREAT DOCUMENTS OF AMERICAN HISTORY: 1775-1865, Edited by John Grafton. (0-486-41124-9)

INCIDENTS IN THE LIFE OF A SLAVE GIRL, Harriet Jacobs. (0-486-41931-2)

GREAT SPEECHES, Abraham Lincoln. (0-486-26872-1)

THE WIT AND WISDOM OF ABRAHAM LINCOLN: A Book of Quotations, Abraham Lincoln. Edited by Bob Blaisdell. (0-486-44097-4)

THE SECOND TREATISE OF GOVERNMENT AND A LETTER CONCERNING TOLERATION, John Locke. (0-486-42464-2)

THE PRINCE, Niccolò Machiavelli. (0-486-27274-5)

MICHEL DE MONTAIGNE: Selected Essays, Michel de Montaigne. Translated by Charles Cotton. Edited by William Carew Hazlitt. (0-486-48603-6)

UTOPIA, Sir Thomas More. (0-486-29583-4)

BEYOND GOOD AND EVIL: Prelude to a Philosophy of the Future, Friedrich Nietzsche. (0-486-29868-X)

TWELVE YEARS A SLAVE, Solomon Northup. (0-486-78962-4)

COMMON SENSE, Thomas Paine. (0-486-29602-4)

BOOK OF AFRICAN-AMERICAN QUOTATIONS, Edited by Joslyn Pine. (0-486-47589-1)

THE TRIAL AND DEATH OF SOCRATES: Four Dialogues, Plato. (0-486-27066-1)

THE REPUBLIC, Plato. (0-486-41121-4)

SIX GREAT DIALOGUES: Apology, Crito, Phaedo, Phaedrus, Symposium, The Republic, Plato. Translated by Benjamin Jowett. (0-486-45465-7)

WOMEN'S WIT AND WISDOM: A Book of Quotations, Edited by Susan L. Rattiner. (0-486-41123-0)

GREAT SPEECHES, Franklin Delano Roosevelt. (0-486-40894-9)

THE CONFESSIONS OF ST. AUGUSTINE, St. Augustine. (0-486-42466-9)

A MODEST PROPOSAL AND OTHER SATIRICAL WORKS, Jonathan Swift. (0-486-28759-9)

THE IMITATION OF CHRIST, Thomas à Kempis. Translated by Aloysius Croft and Harold Bolton. (0-486-43185-1)

CIVIL DISOBEDIENCE AND OTHER ESSAYS, Henry David Thoreau. (0-486-27563-9)

WALDEN; OR, LIFE IN THE WOODS, Henry David Thoreau. (0-486-28495-6)

NARRATIVE OF SOJOURNER TRUTH, Sojourner Truth. (0-486-29899-X)

THE WIT AND WISDOM OF MARK TWAIN: A Book of Quotations, Mark Twain. (0-486-40664-4)

UP FROM SLAVERY, Booker T. Washington. (0-486-28738-6)

A VINDICATION OF THE RIGHTS OF WOMAN, Mary Wollstonecraft. (0-486-29036-0)

PLAYS

THE ORESTEIA TRILOGY: Agamemnon, the Libation-Bearers and the Furies, Aeschylus. (0-486-29242-8)

EVERYMAN, Anonymous. (0-486-28726-2)

THE BIRDS, Aristophanes. (0-486-40886-8)

LYSISTRATA, Aristophanes. (0-486-28225-2)

THE CHERRY ORCHARD, Anton Chekhov. (0-486-26682-6)

THE SEA GULL, Anton Chekhov. (0-486-40656-3)

MEDEA, Euripides. (0-486-27548-5)

FAUST, PART ONE, Johann Wolfgang von Goethe. (0-486-28046-2)

THE INSPECTOR GENERAL, Nikolai Gogol. (0-486-28500-6)

SHE STOOPS TO CONQUER, Oliver Goldsmith. (0-486-26867-5)

GHOSTS, Henrik Ibsen. (0-486-29852-3)

A DOLL'S HOUSE, Henrik Ibsen. (0-486-27062-9)

HEDDA GABLER, Henrik Ibsen. (0-486-26469-6)

DR. FAUSTUS, Christopher Marlowe. (0-486-28208-2)

TARTUFFE, Molière. (0-486-41117-6)

BEYOND THE HORIZON, Eugene O'Neill. (0-486-29085-9)

THE EMPEROR JONES, Eugene O'Neill. (0-486-29268-1)

CYRANO DE BERGERAC, Edmond Rostand. (0-486-41119-2)

MEASURE FOR MEASURE: Unabridged, William Shakespeare. (0-486-40889-2)

FOUR GREAT TRAGEDIES: Hamlet, Macbeth, Othello, and Romeo and Juliet, William Shakespeare. (0-486-44083-4)

THE COMEDY OF ERRORS, William Shakespeare. (0-486-42461-8)

HENRY V, William Shakespeare. (0-486-42887-7)

MUCH ADO ABOUT NOTHING, William Shakespeare. (0-486-28272-4)

FIVE GREAT COMEDIES: Much Ado About Nothing, Twelfth Night, A Midsummer Night's Dream, As You Like It and The Merry Wives of Windsor, William Shakespeare. (0-486-44086-9)

OTHELLO, William Shakespeare. (0-486-29097-2)

AS YOU LIKE IT, William Shakespeare. (0-486-40432-3)

ROMEO AND JULIET, William Shakespeare. (0-486-27557-4)

A MIDSUMMER NIGHT'S DREAM, William Shakespeare. (0-486-27067-X)

THE MERCHANT OF VENICE, William Shakespeare. (0-486-28492-1)

HAMLET, William Shakespeare. (0-486-27278-8)

RICHARD III, William Shakespeare. (0-486-28747-5)

PLAYS

THE TAMING OF THE SHREW, William Shakespeare. (0-486-29765-9)

MACBETH, William Shakespeare. (0-486-27802-6)

KING LEAR, William Shakespeare. (0-486-28058-6)

FOUR GREAT HISTORIES: Henry IV Part I, Henry IV Part II, Henry V, and Richard III, William Shakespeare. (0-486-44629-8)

THE TEMPEST, William Shakespeare. (0-486-40658-X)

JULIUS CAESAR, William Shakespeare. (0-486-26876-4)

TWELFTH NIGHT; OR, WHAT YOU WILL, William Shakespeare. (0-486-29290-8)

HEARTBREAK HOUSE, George Bernard Shaw. (0-486-29291-6)

PYGMALION, George Bernard Shaw. (0-486-28222-8)

ARMS AND THE MAN, George Bernard Shaw. (0-486-26476-9)

OEDIPUS REX, Sophocles. (0-486-26877-2)

ANTIGONE, Sophocles. (0-486-27804-2)

FIVE GREAT GREEK TRAGEDIES, Sophocles, Euripides and Aeschylus. (0-486-43620-9)

THE FATHER, August Strindberg. (0-486-43217-3)

THE PLAYBOY OF THE WESTERN WORLD AND RIDERS TO THE SEA, J. M. Synge. (0-486-27562-0)

TWELVE CLASSIC ONE-ACT PLAYS, Edited by Mary Carolyn Waldrep. (0-486-47490-9)

LADY WINDERMERE'S FAN, Oscar Wilde. (0-486-40078-6)

AN IDEAL HUSBAND, Oscar Wilde. (0-486-41423-X)

THE IMPORTANCE OF BEING EARNEST, Oscar Wilde. (0-486-26478-5)